WITNESS

TO VICTORY

The Final Book
of
Witness to Revolution

MICHAEL & JENNIFER CECERE

HERITAGE BOOKS
2024

HERITAGE BOOKS
AN IMPRINT OF HERITAGE BOOKS, INC.

Books, CDs, and more—Worldwide

For our listing of thousands of titles see our website
at
www.HeritageBooks.com

Published 2024 by
HERITAGE BOOKS, INC.
Publishing Division
5810 Ruatan Street
Berwyn Heights, MD 20740

Cover art: Painting *Surrender of Lord Cornwallis* by John Trumbull

International Standard Book Number
Paperbound: 978-0-7884-2858-6

Table of Contents

Acknowledgements

This book, like the two that preceded it, was written in collaboration with my daughter, Jennifer. The direction of all three books has been rather easy to determine. We've just followed the history of the American Revolution. I have a firm grasp on that material, but it is Jennifer, with her keen editorial eye and more importantly, her superb writing skills, who makes the story come alive with vivid description and detail. I am very grateful for her guidance, time, and hard work.

My friends at Colonial Williamsburg also deserve recognition for their steadfast dedication to telling America's past in an authentic manner. There is no better place in the world to inspire folks about the American Revolution than Colonial Williamsburg, and I appreciate all that the foundation and its wonderful people do. The fine folks at Heritage Books were also very helpful, especially Debbie Riley who helped edit the book.

I (Jennifer) am also incredibly grateful to my daughter, Lyla, who put up with my hours and hours of writing. This book would have taken much, much longer to complete if she were not such a wonderful, easygoing baby.

About the Authors

Michael Cecere is a retired History teacher who resides in Williamsburg, Virginia with his wife, Susan. Originally from Maine, he taught high school and college level American History for thirty years in Virginia. The author of twenty-five books and numerous articles on the American Revolution and Revolutionary War, he continues to research and write in retirement.

When he is not writing, Mr. Cecere volunteers and works at Colonial Williamsburg, sometimes as a tobacco farmer, other times as a soldier or a colonial dancer. He also participates in Revolutionary War reenactments throughout the east coast and lectures at historic sites and historical societies.

Jennifer Cecere Miyazaki is a passionate writer like her father, but until now, has kept her writing mostly to herself. She grew up in Virginia but has spent the majority of her post-university life in Tokyo, Japan, where she now resides with her husband, their dog, and daughter. In addition to her love of writing, she enjoys teaching—particularly children—and has spent the past decade inspiring young learners to follow their dreams.

When she is not writing or teaching, she can be found having long-distance conversations with her family, out in nature with her family, or on the couch with a book in hand.

Introduction

This is the last of three books that we hope will enlighten readers about the American Revolution and Revolutionary War. Written as historical fiction about the lives of three young people growing up in Williamsburg, Virginia during the Revolution, great effort has been made to present their stories as historically accurate as possible.

Our hope is that readers will develop a stronger understanding and appreciation of the American Revolution and the struggle and sacrifice it took to secure our independence as a nation.

The first book, *Witness to Revolution*, spanned the years 1771 through 1777 and explored critical events that led to America's declaration of independence. The outbreak of war in 1775 and the events that followed impacted every Virginian, and our main characters, brothers James and John Southall, and their friend Rebecca Anderson—three children growing up in Williamsburg—witnessed it all.

In the second book, *Witness to War*, James, John, and Rebecca are teenagers living in a new nation that is three years into its war for independence. The war is distant, happening mostly in the north, but seems to be getting closer with each passing season, especially for James and John, who turn sixteen—the age of compulsory militia service—in December of 1778 and 1779 respectively. James serves in the militia, and John, the Continental army, each participating in the war just as Rebecca feared. The war touches Rebecca and her family as well when they leave Williamsburg in 1780 and relocate to Virginia's new capital, Richmond.

In the third and final book, James, John, and Rebecca are swept up in the critical events of 1781 as the war intensifies in the south. John is with General Nathanael Greene's army in the Carolinas and participates in the crucial battles of Cowpens, Guilford Courthouse, Hobkirk's Hill and Ninety-Six.

James and Rebecca must deal with a British invasion of Virginia, first by the American traitor Benedict Arnold, who burns part of the new capital, Richmond, and then occupies Portsmouth. Then by General William Phillips, who briefly occupies Williamsburg and defeats the Virginians at Petersburg. And finally, by General Charles Cornwallis, who arrives in May, assumes command of the seven thousand British troops in Virginia, runs roughshod through the central part of the state, occupies Williamsburg for nearly two weeks, and ends up at Yorktown.

James, John, and Rebecca were all participants and witnesses to the crucial events of 1781 that occurred in the south. This third and final book focuses on their journey through the tumultuous, exciting year.

Chapter One

Arnold Invades Virginia

Eighteen-year-old James Southall welcomed the start of 1781 with the person he was most fond of in the world—Rebecca Anderson. They had been friends for a decade, growing up as neighbors in Virginia's colonial capital, Williamsburg. But as they'd grown older, their friendship had blossomed into romance, and now, the pair was very much in love with one another.

Tall and lean with long brown hair tied back in a cue, James was the eldest son of tavernkeepers in Williamsburg. He was also a graduate of the college of William and Mary, an accomplishment that had landed him a tutoring position to the children of General Thomas Nelson in Yorktown.

James had managed to impress General Nelson, who served as the overall commander of Virginia's militia, to such a degree that the general had made him an aide-de-camp in the fall of 1780. While James was honored to have been chosen by General Nelson, it only rooted him deeper in Yorktown, and thus further away from Rebecca.

In the beginning, the separation hadn't been too bad. James kept busy with tutoring, and Rebecca was kept busy by the guests at her father's tavern and by her little sister, Hope, whom Rebecca had been trying to tutor. But then in the spring of 1780, Virginia's leaders moved the capital from Williamsburg to Richmond, a move that Mr. Anderson knew would negatively impact his business. And with a family to provide for… well, he couldn't allow that to happen.

So, when the capital moved to Richmond, the Anderson family followed. And luckily, it proved to be a smart decision, as Mr. Anderson's new tavern was quite prosperous.

But Richmond was much further from Williamsburg than Yorktown. Only twelve miles stood between Williamsburg and Yorktown, making it relatively easy for James to come and visit Rebecca during his longer breaks. Richmond, on the other hand, was some sixty miles from Yorktown—a trip that was much more difficult to make. James and Rebecca had only managed to see each other twice after her move to Richmond in 1780.

The Christmas season of 1780 was one such visit. The celebration of Christmas in the 18th century was a twelve-day affair that began on Christmas Day and continued until Twelfth Night on January 5th. It was a time for feasts and family, and a time that everyone cherished more than usual due to the anxiety and weariness six years of war had brought on.

James and Rebecca huddled together in front of a roaring fire as they waited to ring in the new year. The firelight made Rebecca's red hair seem almost molten. James took a strand of it and tucked it behind her ear, watching the flames dance in her blue eyes.

"Do you think John had a merry birthday?" she asked him, her eyes on the fire.

John was James's younger brother, and on New Year's Eve of 1780, he was just a few days into his 17th year. Though the brothers were similar in appearance, their personalities couldn't be more different. John had never shared James's burning desire for knowledge, had never been able to sit still long enough to learn much of anything from a book. Not that he wasn't intelligent—he was, just, in his own way. John had always been the more energetic, outgoing brother. And from a young age he found himself yearning for action and adventure, eager to join the fight for American independence. So just a few months after his 16th birthday, he had enlisted in the Continental army—much to Rebecca's chagrin.

James could tell Rebecca was worried about John. The three of them had been the best of friends for ten years, inseparable until the war came and reshaped their lives. And the last letter they had received from John had not been filled with the cheeriest of news. John had survived the battles he'd been in, but he was far away from his family and friends, encamped with a weak and demoralized American army along a river in South Carolina.

James reached for Rebecca's hand and gave it a gentle squeeze. "I think John probably had a wonderful birthday. He likely announced it to everyone at the camp, so he surely received countless well wishes."

A small smile crossed Rebecca's face. It was not hard to picture John gloating about the camp, humming "Happy Birthday" to himself—loudly. Still, he was so far away, and in a war camp. *Is it possible to be happy in a place like that?* Rebecca wondered.

"Don't worry about John, Becca," James said to her. "He'll be alright, and he'll come back to us."

Rebecca wasn't so sure, but she nodded. "I just hope the war ends soon," she whispered as she nuzzled closer to James. "That this will be the last year of violence and chaos."

But as James and Rebecca bid farewell to 1780 and started to dream of a brighter year ahead, a rumor reached Richmond of a large, unidentified fleet off Virginia's coast. When no further word of the fleet arrived the following day, everyone—including Governor Thomas Jefferson—assumed there was nothing to worry about.

They were wrong.

Brigadier-General Benedict Arnold, the notorious American traitor, had arrived in Virginia with a small fleet and fourteen hundred British troops. James and Rebecca had been out for an afternoon stroll along the river when they learned of their arrival, only two days into the new year.

A man had rushed past them, his eyes wide with panic. James and Rebecca exchanged a look, but had no time for words as another man dashed by. "They're sailing up the river," the man cried to them in warning. "Thirty ships or more!"

James and Rebecca hurried home where Mr. Anderson confirmed that he too had heard the news. "The Governor received a dispatch this morning that a British fleet was making its way up the river," Mr. Anderson said. "They could be heading for Williamsburg, or Petersburg, or," he swallowed, "here."

Richmond would make the most sense, James thought. He squeezed Rebecca's hand and then left for his room to pack his clothes. "I must be off immediately, General Nelson will expect me," he said as he started to walk away.

As an aide to General Nelson with the rank of lieutenant, it was James's duty to return to the general as quickly as possible, so he was surprised when Mr. Anderson shook his head. "You need to delay your departure, son. Governor Jefferson has called for assistance to evacuate the city. I'm on my way to help now."

Mr. Anderson held the rank of major in the militia, although his recent move to Richmond had left him with no troops to command. Nevertheless, the Governor had called for help, and Major Anderson answered the call.

James reached once more for Rebecca, tightening his grasp on her hands as he took in her creased brows and frown. "Everything will be alright," he said. "It's just a precaution. They likely won't come this far up. I'll be back with your father soon enough," he assured her before leaving with Major Anderson.

Rebecca stood in the doorway with her mother and watched them go. "It'll be alright," she said as she turned to her mother. "Even if they're coming, they're still a long way off."

Her mother gave a tight smile but nodded. "Yes, yes," she said quietly. "It'll all be alright."

James and Major Anderson hurried down to the river where they found chests full of government documents stacked on the shore. Barrels of gunpowder, casks of musket balls and flints, and crates full of muskets were also stacked along the river, all waiting to be ferried across.

"Major Anderson!" called out Colonel George Muter, the Commissioner of the War Office. "I need you to attend to the removal of these items across the river while I seek Governor Jefferson."

"Of course, Colonel," replied Major Anderson. "How may Lieutenant Southall help?"

Muter looked James up and down. "He is to come with me."

James followed Colonel Muter toward Governor Jefferson's residence. "Are you Colonel Southall's son?" he asked.

"I am, sir," replied James.

"I imagine your father has his hands full at the moment," continued Colonel Muter. "This fleet caught everyone by surprise."

James thought of his family in Williamsburg and wished he could be there to help. His father was a colonel of militia there, and had undoubtedly taken the field in response to the alarm.

When the two reached Jefferson's residence, they were escorted in by a servant. The governor was seated at his desk, furiously scribbling dispatches to call out the militia from nearby counties.

"Colonel Muter, how goes the evacuation?" Governor Jefferson asked, not bothering to look up.

"We're making slow progress, sir," replied Muter. "But I have Lieutenant Southall here to assist in the transport of your papers, sir."

Governor Jefferson looked up from his desk. "Southall? Would that be Colonel Southall's son from Williamsburg?"

"Indeed, sir, it is I," replied James, stepping forward.

"Well, sir, you have grown considerably since I last saw you at Mr. Wythe's. I appreciate your assistance."

James nodded in acknowledgement. "I am at your service, sir."

"Before we proceed with my papers, help me complete these dispatches. Come, sit at that desk," said Jefferson, pointing to a small desk in the corner. "I need several more copies of this dispatch for the counties above Richmond."

James did as he was told and wrote out five copies of the governor's order to call out the militia. When he was finished, Governor Jefferson led James to an adjoining room and motioned to various stacks of books and papers strewn about. "All of this needs to be packed up and sent across the river. Can you attend to that, Mr. Southall?"

"Certainly, sir," replied James, disappointed that the governor had forgotten he was a lieutenant.

"Benjamin!" Mr. Jefferson called, summoning one of his enslaved servants. "Assist Mr. Southall with packing these papers and those in the other room."

Benjamin replied with a bow. “Yes, sir,” he said as he turned to retrieve several trunks for the purpose.

“I must escort my family in Tuckahoe, and may not return until tomorrow,” Jefferson announced. “So let us delay the transport of the documents across the river until tomorrow.”

“Of course, sir,” replied James with a bow. He scanned the trove of documents before him and thought of General Nelson once more—surely, he would be expecting him. But James glanced at the overwhelmed governor again and thought better of mentioning his desire to return to Nelson’s side. *Governor Jefferson clearly needs assistance as well,* he thought.

By sunset, the trunks had been filled and stacked in the central passage, allowing James to return to the river to see if his assistance was needed there.

To no one’s surprise, it was, and James ended up crossing the river several times to supervise the transport of fabric, food, muskets, and gunpowder.

Colonel Muter paused the crossings at 7p.m., however, when it grew stormy and too dangerous to continue. He instructed Major Anderson and James to return at sunrise. The pair agreed and rushed back to the tavern, where

Rebecca and Mrs. Anderson greeted them, eager to learn the latest news.

"What is happening, Robert?" asked Mrs. Anderson. "Will we have to flee?"

"I don't know, dear," he answered truthfully. "They are taking precautions in case we have to, but no one knows for sure that the British are coming to Richmond."

"Well, what about us?" continued Mrs. Anderson. "Should we prepare also?"

Mr. Anderson paused to consider. Finally, he met his wife's eyes and nodded. "We probably should," he said softly. "We probably should."

Mrs. Anderson could see the worry and exhaustion etched on her husband's face, so she said no more on the subject. But she realized that whatever preparations the family needed to make would likely fall to her—Mr. Anderson would be away, after all. This concerned her, because she felt quite poorly and knew she was coming down with something. She vowed to keep her worries to herself, however. Mr. Anderson had enough to worry about already.

After Mr. and Mrs. Anderson turned in for the night, James and Rebecca remained at the dining table, both too anxious to sleep.

Rebecca was chewing on one of her fingernails. “What’s going to happen, James?” she asked nervously.

“I don’t know,” he replied. “We have to return to the river tomorrow to finish moving supplies across. And I need to join General Nelson as soon as I can, so I shall likely leave tomorrow.”

Rebecca let out a heavy sigh and James noticed her eyes grow misty. “A general’s aide is a pretty safe job,” he added, “so you needn’t worry about me.”

Rebecca smiled and reached her hand out to hold his.

“What of you?” asked James. “If you have to flee, where will you go?”

“I don’t know… Uncle James is here, but if the British come, they will likely burn his foundry. Outside of him, we have no family here, so I don’t know where we would go.”

James frowned with concern, but did not want to further upset Rebecca, so he replaced it quickly with a crooked grin. “Well, it is likely they won’t come this far upriver anyway. They are more likely to go to Williamsburg, or perhaps Petersburg.”

Rebecca let out a small gasp, her hand flying to her mouth. "What of your family?" she breathed. "What will become of them if they burn Williamsburg?"

"We have property outside of town they can go to," James said reassuringly. "They're probably there right now."

Rebecca's shoulders relaxed, but the fear remained in her eyes. "Blast this cursed war," she muttered. "I knew we wouldn't escape it."

"Calm yourself," James hushed. "It's probably just another raid. They'll likely be gone within a few weeks."

Rebecca wrung her hands. "I pray you're right."

Neither wanted to turn in for the evening, but as the candles burned down, James announced he needed to be up at dawn to return to the river—he needed sleep.

"Wake me before you leave," Rebecca said as they rose to hug each other goodnight.

"I will," promised James, kissing her on the cheek.

The morning dawned cold and gloomy, and by mid-morning, James was soaked through by a light rain that stubbornly lingered. The rain slowed their progress across the river and before he knew it, most of the day had passed.

At 3 p.m. Governor Jefferson arrived and James mustered up the courage to ask if he might be relieved from the remainder of his duty to return to General Nelson.

"Of course, of course," replied Governor Jefferson. "And on your journey, you can do me a great service by delivering a message to Speaker Harrison in Berkeley."

James smiled uncomfortably, knowing that a stop at Berkeley would delay his progress to Williamsburg, but he agreed to deliver the message and returned to Mr. Anderson's tavern to prepare for his journey, and to say goodbye to Rebecca.

"You be careful, James. And write to me when you can," Rebecca said as they embraced in the doorway.

"I shall, I shall," he promised her.

Their embrace was interrupted by Mr. Anderson, who had rushed toward them, hands waving. "Come now, Rebecca, he must be on his way."

Mounting the horse that General Nelson had provided James for his trip, Spartan, he left Richmond before sundown, riding hard until it grew too dark to do so. He reached Berkeley, some twenty-five miles downriver, before 9 p.m., and was greeted by Speaker Harrison.

"You look familiar to me, sir," Speaker Harrison mused after James delivered the dispatch.

"I am Lieutenant Southall, sir," said James with a bow. "We have met several times at my father's tavern in Williamsburg."

"Yes, of course," replied Speaker Harrison. "I hope your family is well."

"As do I," replied James. "They were when I last saw them before Christmas, but with the enemy coming upriver, I fear for their safety."

"I'm sure they are fine, lad," Speaker Harrison said warmly as he opened the dispatch. "Your father is a clever man."

Speaker Harrison read the dispatch and nodded in agreement before looking back up at James. "You must be tired, son. Will you take some refreshment?"

"Thank you, sir, but I must be off. I am overdue to rejoin General Nelson."

Speaker Harrison voiced his understanding and let James continue on his way. Around 10 p.m., James reached Charles City Courthouse and noticed a handful of men gathered outside a tavern across from it. As he approached,

James heard cannon fire from the direction of the river and tensed.

"Where are you off to, lad?" asked one of the men suspiciously, grabbing hold of Spartan's reins.

"I'm riding to join General Nelson," James said. "I'm his aide, but was in Richmond when all of this started." His gaze darted toward the river. "What do you make of the cannon?"

The man loosened his grip on Spartan's reins, seemingly convinced that James was telling the truth. "We're not sure," he replied, following James's gaze. "Could be the fort across the river at Hood's Point."

James wanted to ride on, but he knew he should investigate the cannon fire, so he asked how to get to the river. Two men stepped forward and said it was just a few miles away and that they would take him there. They mounted horses and led James to the river. When they reached it, James was shocked at what he saw.

The river was full of ships anchored just below Hood's Point, where a fort with several large cannons had been built on the other side of the James River. Most of the cannon fire was coming from the ships, but occasionally a blast could be heard from Hood's Point. From what James could tell, neither side did much damage to the other, but James noticed numerous longboats full of troops rowing toward the opposite shore and realized that Hood's Point was likely doomed. He also realized that he had to head back to Richmond as quickly as possible to warn Governor Jefferson.

"We must be off," he announced to his guides. "I must report what has occurred."

James pushed Spartan as hard as he dared in the darkness for Richmond, covering nearly forty miles in five hours. He arrived at Governor Jefferson's residence before 5 a.m. and pounded on the door.

"It's Lieutenant Southall with urgent intelligence for Governor Jefferson," he announced breathlessly to the enslaved man who answered the door. "I must see him *immediately*."

James waited in the central passage while Governor Jefferson was informed of his arrival. The governor came down the stairs wearing a colorful banyan (robe), his hair uncombed.

"What is it, Lieutenant Southall? What is so urgent?"

"Sir, the enemy was at Hood's Point just a few hours ago. I expect they have seized it by now and have advanced further up the river. I saw them attack the point myself, sir."

"Then they are meant for here or Petersburg," replied Jefferson. The governor looked away for a moment, placing a hand on his chin, his brows furrowed. "In either case, we must prepare for them. I need you to awaken Major Anderson and tell him to alarm the officers, he knows who they are. Can you do that, lad?"

"Certainly, sir."

"Good, then off with you." Jefferson turned quickly to go upstairs, calling for Benjamin—his personal servant—as he did so.

James departed and rode to the Anderson's tavern, just a half mile away, and awakened the sleeping family. Unaware of the unfolding situation, Major Anderson scolded James for making such a fuss. "By God, James! Must you be so loud? Mrs. Anderson is not well."

"Forgive me, sir, but I have urgent news and a message from Governor Jefferson. The British have reached Hood's Point and are likely past it by now. The Governor asks that you inform the other militia officers."

The color drained from Major Anderson's face. "This is not good," he muttered to himself. "There aren't enough men here." He looked up suddenly and realized that Rebecca heard him—he had not noticed her standing in the doorway, her face now as ashen as his.

"But they're probably meant for Petersburg," he said in an attempt to relieve her worry. "It's a much more valuable target than Richmond."

Major Anderson looked back to James. "You must be exhausted, son. And I'm sure your horse can go no further. Take a room upstairs and rest."

"I shall attend to him, Father," Rebecca said as she stepped forward to take James by the hand. "Sarah, fetch a basin of water and bring it upstairs. Will, start a fire in the first bedchamber." Rebecca then led James, whose nerves had finally calmed enough to make room for the utter exhaustion surging through him, toward the stairs.

"What is to happen, James?" she whispered as they walked together upstairs.

"I'm not sure," he whispered back. "But there is likely to be a fight."

A plate of cold ham, bread, and a mug of cider were brought to James, and he gratefully consumed it all. As he ate, Rebecca wrung her hands over and over again, anxious that in just a few hours the British could be on her doorstep.

James looked out the window and noticed it had started to rain hard. "Ah," he said, hoping to ease Rebecca's nervousness. "They won't get very far with that rain pelting them. We've got some time yet."

"But it only took you a few hours to get here."

"Yes, but I was riding hard on Spartan, and they likely won't have many horses. They'll have to march on foot, and this rain will turn the road into a bog. It could be days before they arrive—assuming they're coming at all."

Rebecca took a deep breath and exhaled. "Well, good then." She walked toward James and took him by the hand. "Plenty of time for you to get some rest," she said as she led him to the bed, pushing him backwards onto it.

James sat up on the edge of the bed and smiled. He wanted Rebecca to stay, but he was exhausted and knew he needed sleep.

"I shall see you in a few hours, Lieutenant Southall," Rebecca said as she turned to leave. When she got to the door she turned to him one last time, her voice soft and low. "Rest well, James. I'm glad you're back."

She left the room and shut the door. James was asleep before she could reach the bottom of the stairs.

Chapter Two

It Is to Be Richmond

James awakened with a start a little after one o' clock in the afternoon. His portmanteau had been brought to his room while he slept, so he shaved, got dressed, and then headed downstairs. He noticed the rain had eased, which was worrying, but he kept his concern to himself.

Rebecca had heard James come down the stairs and emerged from her parents' bedroom. Her younger sister, Hope, followed behind her.

"How's your mother?" James asked.

"She's resting," Rebecca answered.

"She's quite ill," added Hope.

"I'm sorry to hear," he said. He wondered about Mr. Anderson's whereabouts as well, but given the news about Mrs. Anderson, feared it would now be rude to ask.

Thankfully, Rebecca seemed able to read his mind. "Father is with the militia at the courthouse," she said. "He's been out all morning."

Just then the door opened and Major Anderson entered.

"Is there any news, Father?" asked Rebecca.

He shook his head. "The last report was from James, hours ago. The militia have been sent home until more is known. How's your mother?"

"She's still very feverish, but is sleeping now," replied Rebecca.

"Has she eaten anything?"

"Nothing," replied Rebecca.

"She tossed and turned a lot, Father," Hope said.

"But she's settled now," continued Rebecca, "and it's best we let her sleep."

Major Anderson nodded in reply. "Let us proceed with dinner without her then," he announced.

James was uncertain about staying. He still felt a duty to return to General Nelson, and now felt rested enough to do so—but he knew his horse was still likely tired from the long night, and the weather remained bleak. He mulled it over a bit longer—Rebecca's hopeful smile chipping away at his resolve—before finally deciding to stay for dinner.

It was served earlier than usual, at two o' clock, because Major Anderson was famished. The conversation at the table focused on what to do if the British should arrive.

"I think we should remain here," Rebecca declared. "Mother is too ill to travel, especially in this rain. We should stay put for her sake. And if we stay, we can better protect the tavern." She noted James's eyebrows rise suddenly at that. "I don't mean fight," she clarified, "but the redcoats will be less likely to steal from us if we are here."

James agreed with Rebecca's reasoning, but feared for her safety if she remained in Richmond. "You're probably right, Becca. But I still think it would be safer if you all left the town."

"But where would we go? We know no one outside this town, and Mother is too ill to travel."

Major Anderson nodded grudgingly in agreement. "I'm afraid Rebecca is right," he sighed. "Mrs. Anderson is too ill to leave. I shall ask Doctor Galt to stay should the British come."

At the end of dinner, a messenger arrived with troubling news that the British had landed at Westover, the estate of the late William Byrd, a mere twenty-five miles away.

Then it is to be Richmond, thought James, his stomach sinking.

Major Anderson realized this as well and told his daughters it was time to prepare for the British. "We must gather and hide our valuables. Bring the silver from the pantry and your mother's jewelry to the office. Also, anything of yours you want to hide." The girls dashed away to comply.

Major Anderson turned back to the messenger. "Tell Colonel Syme that Lieutenant Southall and I will be with him within the half hour." He then turned to James. "Go pack your things and meet me in the stable."

James did as he was told, though he had little to pack—just a dirty shirt, breeches, and stockings.

Rebecca intercepted him at the foot of the stairs after he had finished, her hands full of silverware. Hope followed behind her with two silver candlesticks and several silver punch ladles.

"I should have had your clothes washed while you slept," Rebecca lamented. "Well, never mind. I can at least see that you take some food with you. Wait here."

She continued to the office to give her father the silver. He placed it all in a sack. Rebecca then ducked into her parents' room and returned with a small jewelry box, which was also placed in the sack. Lastly, her father added a small leather pouch full of paper currency and a few coins.

"I'm going to put this in the stable under the manure pile," explained Mr. Anderson. "Hand me that other sack." Rebecca did so and her father placed the sack of valuables inside the second sack and tied it up. He then handed Rebecca his ledger book and told her to take it to the kitchen and have Sally, the Anderson's enslaved cook, hide it upstairs in her quarters.

Rebecca dashed off with the book, grabbing James, who had remained in the hallway at the bottom of the stairs, on the way. "Come with me to the kitchen," she commanded, leading him by the arm.

When they entered the kitchen, Rebecca told Sally to pack up two cloth bags of dried fruit and sweet meat (nuts) for James and her father. Rebecca wrapped a loaf of soft bread in cloth and added a large chunk of cheese to it.

"Here," she said, handing the food to James. "This should get you and Father through supper. Just be sure to come back in the morning for breakfast," she said with a weak smile.

James smiled. “I shall try,” he said, knowing that it was unlikely that he would. He then placed the food down and took Rebecca into his arms. Sally averted her eyes and left the kitchen, giving Rebecca an opportunity to snuggle closer to James.

“Be careful, please be careful,” she pleaded.

“Don’t worry, Becca. I will.”

They heard Major Anderson pass the kitchen on the way to the stables and separated. “I must join your father now,” said James, backing away. “I’ll be back soon.”

Rebecca watched him go to the stables. *Come back to me, please come back to me,* she thought as he disappeared inside the stables. She then turned to Sally and said, “Father needs you to hide this upstairs, Sally. It’s important.” Sally nodded and took the ledger book to her quarters above the kitchen.

Will, one of Major Anderson’s three enslaved men, was adjusting the saddle of Spartan when James entered the stable. Major Anderson was in the next stall, burying the sack of valuables deep into a pile of used, damp straw in the corner. He then went to inspect his horse, which had already been saddled. James secured his portmanteau to the back of Spartan and inspected him as well.

“He’s likely still tired from last night, so don’t push him too hard,” Major Anderson advised. “Only if it’s necessary.”

“Yes, sir,” replied James.

They led their horses to the front and tied them up. Then they both entered the tavern to say their goodbyes. After saying his goodbyes to his wife and youngest daughter, Major Anderson approached Rebecca, his arms outstretched. She walked into his embrace and squeezed him hard. “I’ve sent for Doctor Galt,” he said. “With his care, your mother should be fine. But be sure to look after her and your sister,” he said as he pressed a kiss to her forehead.

“I will,” she said, stepping away. “Be careful, Father. I shall pray for both of you.”

Major Anderson smiled and turned toward the door. James embraced Rebecca one last time and kissed her on the cheek, whispering, “I love you, Becca.”

Rebecca hugged him tighter. “And I love you.”

Rebecca followed James to the door and watched as he and her father mounted their horses and rode toward the church, the muster point for the militia.

"God protect them both," prayed Rebecca under her breath as they faded from view.

When Major Anderson and James reached the church, they found over a hundred men milling about. Colonel Alexander Syme, the commander of Richmond's militia, greeted them.

"Major Anderson, I'm glad to see you. Join us inside. You too," he paused, "Lieutenant," he said to James, clearly having forgotten his name.

Inside the church, several officers were gathered around a map, discussing the route the enemy would likely take to reach Richmond. All agreed that from Westover, they were just a day's march away.

"We need to send some horsemen out to scout," said one of them. Colonel Syme looked to Major Anderson. "Major, you have no troops here, will you and the lieutenant go?"

"Of course," Major Anderson replied. "But as we are unfamiliar with the ground, we could use a guide."

Major Travis Rose cleared his throat. "I shall detach a party of horses from my company and join you," he offered. Major Anderson nodded in acceptance. It was agreed that the scouting party would depart as soon as possible with the two majors commanding jointly.

The sun had almost set by the time they left Richmond. Earlier in the day it had rained hard, so the road was soft and muddy. Thick clouds obscured the moon and stars, and a gusty winter wind chilled men and horse alike.

"If they're coming, they'll make slow progress," Major Anderson said confidently. "I imagine they'll wait until the morning to march, but it's best to be on guard regardless."

The small party of horsemen advanced down River Road toward Westover, their pace slow. James was relieved; he had pushed his horse hard over many miles the previous night. *Go easy now, boy,* he thought to himself as he patted Spartan's neck, *I may need you soon*.

About ten miles from Richmond, they reached a hill overlooking a small bridge and creek. Major Rose suggested that they stop there until daylight. "We don't want to blunder into them in the darkness," he said.

Major Anderson agreed. When one of the soldiers asked if they could build a fire, to help fight the cold, Anderson answered no. "It's too dangerous, lad. They might see it and sneak up on us."

While the others tried to sleep on the cold, wet ground, James offered to take the first watch.

"Very good," replied Major Anderson. "Let us post a man at the bridge and another a hundred yards beyond," he said to Major Rose, who nodded in agreement.

"Wake me at midnight, Lieutenant," Major Anderson said to James. "I'll take the second watch with two others."

"Then I'll take the third," said Major Rose.

The officers dispersed and James sat down under a tree while the others spread their blankets upon the freezing, damp, ground to sleep. James looked at his pocket watch. *It's not even eight yet,* he fretted as he shivered. *It's going to be a long night.*

Major Anderson whispered to James as he settled in, "Be sure to check on the sentries every hour. And do so quietly, we don't want any accidents."

"Yes, sir," James whispered back.

James was surprised how fast the men around him fell asleep. Then he remembered that he had slept for most of the previous day—which was likely why he didn't feel very tired.

He checked the sentries at 9 p.m. The one at the bridge was dismounted and leaning against a tree to block the wind, his horse standing nearby, sleeping. James approached carefully, whispering, "It's Lieutenant Southall," as he drew near.

"I don't think they're coming tonight, sir," said the sentry. "Not on a night such as this."

"You're probably right," James murmured. "But they've surprised us more than once already."

James passed the bridge and headed for the second sentry. He was slumped forward on his horse, and for a moment James thought he was sleeping, but when he stepped on a twig, the sentry spun around and shouted, "Halt!"

James froze, palms up toward the sentry. "Easy now, it's Lieutenant Southall."

James saw the sentry relax, so he drew closer.

"Sorry, sir. I'm a bit jumpy tonight." The sentry ran a hand through his hair, and James noted the youthful roundness of his face—*he couldn't be more than sixteen,* he thought. *Definitely younger than I am.*

"What do you have for a weapon?" asked James.

"Just this saber, sir."

"I'll bring you a pistol on my next round, but be careful," James warned. "We don't want any accidents."

The sentry, who still seemed quite nervous, thanked him and then reported all was quiet. James stayed with him for a few more minutes, knowing company could help ease the boy's nerves. But he couldn't stay forever. "I'll be back in an hour," James whispered and finally headed back to camp.

When he arrived, he took a pistol from Major Anderson's saddle and carefully checked to make sure it was loaded. There were two pistols on Mr. Anderson's saddle, but James only took one. *It's to be a signal,* he thought, *not a weapon.*

James inspected the sentries twice more before waking Major Anderson at midnight as instructed.

"I left one of your pistols with the out sentry," James said.

"Good thinking. Now let's go relieve those two with these," continued Major Anderson, pointing to the two men sleeping nearby.

James was back at camp under a blanket by 12:30 a.m. With the wet ground and cold air, he didn't think he'd manage to sleep, but he did, for the next thing he knew, Major Anderson was shaking him. "James, James, time to get up. Come on, lad."

It was still dark, but the first light of day was starting to appear on the horizon. One of the men, teeth chattering, asked Major Rose if he could start a fire now. “I don’t see why not,” said Major Rose, surveying the sunrise. “It’s nearly dawn.” Major Anderson frowned at the decision but said nothing. The men broke dead branches and twigs from the trees, and within a few minutes had a small fire going.

As they gathered around it to warm themselves, a pistol shot rang out from the direction of the out sentry.

“Mount up, boys!” commanded Major Anderson. “We have guests!”

The fire was kicked out and the men scrambled to get their gear. It was light enough now to see the sentry who had fired the alarm, riding hard for the bridge. The sentry at the bridge mounted his horse and together they both galloped toward the encampment.

“What did you see?” asked Major Anderson when they arrived.

“Horsemen coming this way,” the sentry replied in a rush.

“Hurry, boys, they’ll likely be on us soon,” Major Anderson called.

"Wait!" Major Rose shouted. "I know those fellas." He pointed toward a party of horsemen dressed in green uniforms who had crested the far hill where the out sentry had been.

"I think those are Colonel Lee's men," said Rose, referring to the cavalry of Light Horse Harry Lee's Legion. "They must have ridden over from Petersburg."

Lee had arrived in Virginia with a combined force of cavalry and infantry in December. Lee's force, called a legion, was transferred to the South by General Washington. Major Rose had seen Lee's Legion in Richmond, but had assumed they'd been sent to Petersburg to join the small number of Virginia Continentals encamped there.

What Major Rose did not realize, was Lee's Legion had then proceeded to South Carolina—and the green coated horsemen he now saw on the far hill were the enemy. They were the Queen's Rangers, under Colonel John Simcoe; all American loyalists aside from their commander, who was a British officer.

It was an easy mistake to make since their green coats were nearly identical to Lee's unit, but this mistake would end up costing Major Rose dearly.

Confident that he knew who the green coated men were, Major Rose announced, "Let us ride over and join them."

Major Anderson hesitated. "I'm not sure that's Colonel Lee, Major."

"Of course it is," replied Rose, annoyed at being challenged.

Major Anderson rode alongside Major Rose and leaned toward him, hoping to prevent the rest of the men from hearing their disagreement.

James watched from nearby. Their body language seemed tense. Then, Major Rose suddenly swung his horse around to face the men who were all waiting for a decision.

"Major Anderson will stay here with Lieutenant Southall and two men," he said gruffly. "The rest will follow me." He whirled his horse around and left at a trot toward the green coated horsemen, who remained on the far hill, observing.

James rode up to Major Anderson, who was watching Major Rose leave. "He's going to regret this," said Major Anderson, "just watch."

At first it appeared that Major Anderson had been wrong. The mysterious horsemen seemed to welcome

Major Rose and his men. But then there was a tussle, as weapons were drawn, reins seized, and hands raised in surrender.

"Just as I thought!" muttered Major Anderson. "Damn fool!"

Simcoe's Rangers broke forward at a gallop, chasing after one militia horseman who'd managed to escape. Shots rang out as the desperate man spurred his horse on, the Rangers firing wildly at him.

"What do we do?" asked James.

"We've got to go. Else we'll be caught, too!" replied Major Anderson as he put spur to horse and headed back to Richmond. James and the others followed suit, ashamed that they had done nothing to help their fleeing comrade.

In truth though, there was little they *could* do. The desperate fellow was on his own. He had one advantage, however, and it proved crucial. *His* horse was rested. But the Rangers had ridden most of the night, so their horses were tired. Thus, the Rangers had ended their pursuit in a matter of minutes when the fleeing rebel had started to pull away.

Although the pursuit had ended soon after it had begun, Major Anderson pushed on as quickly as possible to warn Richmond. James kept pace on Spartan, but then caught sight of the fleeing rider behind them and called out to the others. “He got away!”

Major Anderson halted and the small party waited for the lucky soldier to join them. He pulled up hard, leaning on his horse, his left arm dangling at his side where he’d been shot.

“Help him down,” ordered Major Anderson. “And tie a tourniquet around his arm.”

The young man looked weak and pale, but still alert.

“Can you ride on?” asked Major Anderson.

“I think so, sir,” he replied. “But it hurts.”

“I know, lad, I know. You did well to escape. Lieutenant, ride alongside this man and keep an eye on him,” Major Anderson said to James.

Their pace to Richmond was slowed by their injured comrade, but they still managed to arrive before 11 a.m. Major Anderson reported to Colonel Syme at the church that the enemy was just a few hours away.

“How many were there? Who commands them?” Colonel Syme asked.

"I'm not sure, sir," replied Major Anderson. "It was an advance party of horsemen that we encountered. They wore green coats like Colonel Lee's men.

Colonel Syme said nothing, frustrated at the lack of information.

Major Anderson asked permission to take the wounded soldier to his tavern, where he believed Doctor Galt was. James accompanied them and when they arrived, they found Doctor Galt, conversing with Rebecca in the central passage. The air around them seemed to shift, turn leaden and heavy.

"What's the matter?" Major Anderson asked.

Doctor Galt took him by the arm and walked into the dining room. James went to Rebecca and noticed tears in her eyes.

"She's very sick, James. Very sick," whispered Rebecca. "Doctor Galt said to prepare for the worst."

James felt his heart sink.

"If only her fever would break," continued Rebecca. "He's bled her several times, but there's been no change."

The doctor and Major Anderson emerged from the room. "The plan remains the same," announced Major Anderson, his voice tight. "Doctor Galt will remain here and care for your mother. You and Hope are to stay and help. James, take Barnes," he continued with a nod to the wounded man leaning against the wall, "to the back to have the doctor look at him."

As James and the wounded soldier walked past, Mr. Anderson placed his hands on Rebecca's shoulders. "You need to stay strong, Rebecca. Your mother will pull through this."

Rebecca stayed silent, but gave a slight nod as her father turned to go back and talk to the doctor once more.

James returned and went to Rebecca. "Don't worry," he said softly. "Your father is right. She'll pull through."

Rebecca said nothing for a moment, just swiped at her eyes. "And what of the British?" she said finally. "What are we to do when they arrive?"

James hesitated, not wanting to upset her further. "Maybe they *won't* arrive. There didn't seem to be that many of them. And there are hundreds of soldiers at the church ready to fight." He didn't sound very confident, but Rebecca knew he meant well and forced a smile.

Just then, Major Anderson re-emerged. "We must return, James." He kissed Rebecca on the cheek, paused for a moment, then patted her shoulders. “My brave girl, my brave girl.” Then he turned and exited out the front.

James pulled Rebecca in for a hug and whispered, “It will be alright. We’ll stop them, and your mother will pull through.”

“Be careful, James,” was all Rebecca could say.

Map of James River

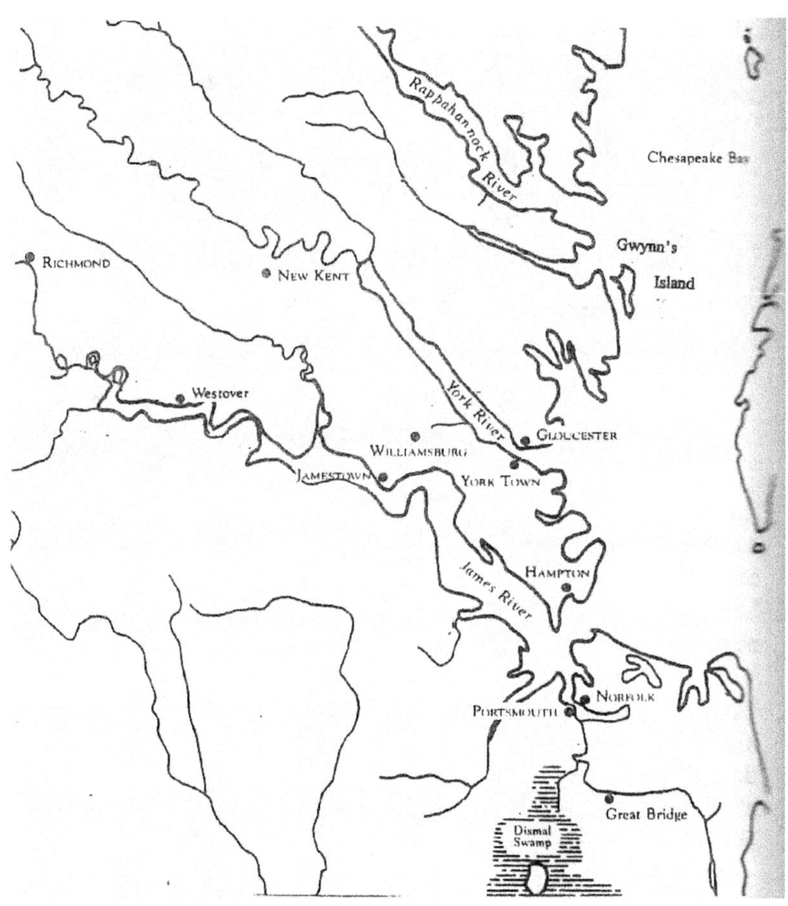

Simcoe's Map of Richmond

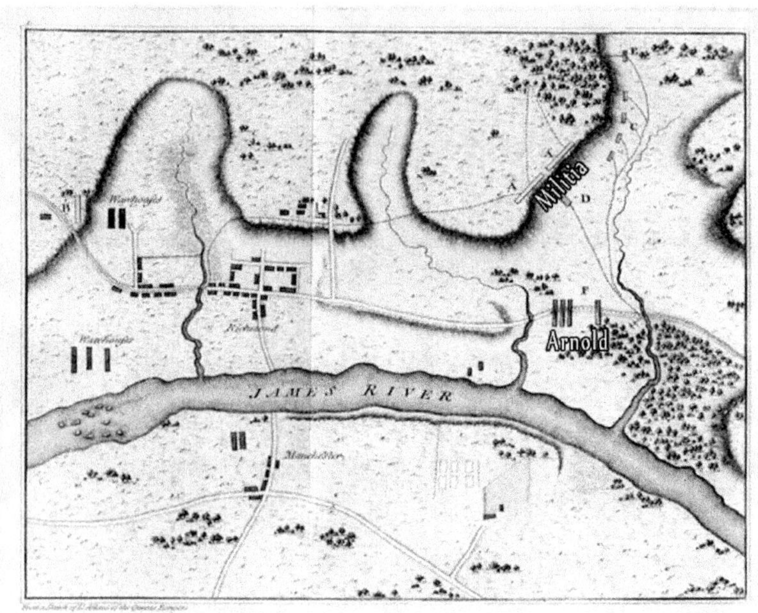

Skirmish at RICHMOND Jan: 5th 1781.

A. Rebel Infantry. B. Rebel Cavalry. C. Queen's Rangers. D. Queens Rangers Cavalry. E. Yagers. F. British Army.

Chapter Three

Why Have you Come Here?

Major Anderson and James hurried back to the church to join the militia that had gathered there, nearly three hundred strong.

"Major Anderson, attend to me, sir," Colonel Syme called out as soon as they entered the church. "I need you to take command of Major Rose's troops."

"Of course, sir," replied Major Anderson. "May I keep Lieutenant Southall with me?"

"Certainly, Major," replied Syme. "You will find Major Rose's men collected outside."

Major Anderson bowed to Colonel Syme and departed with James in tow. When they stopped outside the door, Major Anderson cupped his hands around his mouth and shouted, "Where are Major Rose's men?"

Two officers, both captains, stepped forward and bowed. "They are with us, sir," said one of them. "Captain Markham and Captain Patterson at your service."

Major Anderson nodded in acknowledgment. "I am Major Anderson, and this," he motioned to James, "is Lieutenant Southall. Your companies are attached to me now. Form your men, gentlemen. We need to deploy."

Both captains turned and called for their lieutenants, who in turn instructed their sergeants to form the companies.

James stood alongside Major Anderson, impressed at his commanding presence and confidence. "You'll attend to me, Lieutenant," Major Anderson said to James. "We'll need to mount."

Colonel Syme appeared at the church door and called for Major Dix. "It is time to deploy," he declared. "Your troops will lead the column."

The militia formed into two lines, faced right, and marched east toward the edge of the hill—some half mile away—where they then deployed for battle. Major Anderson's troops were posted on the left of the militia line; Major Dix to his right, overlooking the road that the enemy would likely approach on. The troops stood on the edge of a steep hill, rising nearly one hundred feet from the road.

This is a strong position, thought James, *we might be able to stop them*. He looked to Major Anderson, who was sitting on his horse looking east through a spy glass. "Nothing yet," the major said when he had finished.

But as James looked closer at the road, dread pooled in his stomach. The road the enemy was on went right past the Anderson's tavern. *Why did we leave them there?* he thought. *We should have taken them away.*

An hour passed and James found the wait unbearable. But sometime after noon a shout rang out. "There! They're coming down the road!" James's eyes darted down the road and could just make out mounted troops in green coats leading a column of red.

There's hundreds of them, he thought, horrified. *How can we stop so many?*

As if he had read James's mind, Major Anderson shouted, "Stand firm, boys! That's a steep hill to climb."

Benedict Arnold himself commanded the British force, some eight hundred strong, and he had purposefully stretched his column out to appear larger and more intimidating. The ploy worked—many of the militia on the hill believed over a thousand men were coming after them.

When Arnold noticed the militia on the hill overlooking the road, he halted the column. He turned to Captain Johann Ewald, the German commander of a detachment of German riflemen known as Jagers, and pointed toward the hill. "That looks like a job for your men, Captain Ewald. Drive them from the hill!"

Ewald acknowledged the command and ordered his Jagers to deploy. They were supported by Colonel Simcoe's Rangers, both mounted and dismounted. All struggled to scramble up the steep hill, the horsemen dismounting to lead their horses up.

James stared in awe, transfixed at their approach. Major Anderson's voice snapped him back.

"Make ready! Present! Fire!" commanded Major Anderson, and the left wing of the American militia line fired its first volley.

The enemy disappeared in a haze of smoke and James found himself instinctively parroting Major Anderson's commands. "Reload, boys, quickly! Hold firm. We've staggered them!"

The militia fire had indeed halted the enemy's advance up the hill—but only for a moment. Being veterans of numerous battles, the Jagers and Rangers knew they had only twenty valuable seconds to close on the militia while they reloaded, so they thundered up the hill with a vicious yell. Their aggressiveness unnerved the Virginians, and some broke from the line and fled to the rear.

James waved his saber madly over his head and tried to stop their flight, shouting, "Hold the line! Hold the line! Come back, you cowards!" But it was hopeless. Their flight sparked panic and the militia line broke.

"Get ahead of them and reform them, Lieutenant!" Major Anderson shouted to James. "We've got to reform!" James spurred Spartan and raced toward the church to cut off the men and reform them. He managed to collect twenty or so, and posted them behind a fence on the far side of the hill. He rode back and forth behind them, watching across the field for the enemy, who had paused at the other edge to catch their breath after their steep uphill climb. James noticed Major Anderson to his right with more men, also behind the fence, and the major nodded to James as if to say, "well done."

James knew they couldn't stop the force in front of them, but they could at least make them pay when they crossed the open ground, and he said as much to the men.

"Stand firm, men. Make them pay for the hill!"

The Jagers and Rangers started across cautiously, met by scattered volleys from the few militia who had reformed. The enemy paused their advance to return fire, and a musket ball whizzed past James's ear. "Keep moving! Close on them!" James heard a British officer yell in the distance, and the enemy surged forward with another yell.

It's time to go, thought James. He looked to Major Anderson, who had clearly reached the same conclusion, and both officers yelled, "Withdraw! Withdraw!"

The troops bolted from the fence, heading for the church, leaving James alone for a moment. He turned to ride away, wanting to spur Spartan and ride past the fleeing militia, but he restrained himself and trotted behind the men, praying as he rode, *Please Lord, not in the back, don't let them shoot me in the back,* over and over.

When he got to the church there were few militia to organize—certainly not enough to take on Arnold's men. Most had continued west past the church, done with the fight. When Major Anderson rode up, he told James that there was nothing else to be done here, before starting west himself, hoping to find militia reinforcements willing to strike back at the enemy. James looked down the hill toward the Anderson's tavern, which was obscured from view, but directly in the path of the main British column. *God protect them,* he thought, then spurred Spartan westward in pursuit of Major Anderson.

While the Jagers and Queen's Rangers swept the militia from the hill, General Arnold's main force marched into Richmond. Arnold stopped at the Courthouse and sent detachments amongst the small town. They searched the buildings and found many had been abandoned, but those that hadn't, contained frightened civilians who offered no resistance.

A British officer barged into the Anderson's tavern and confronted Rebecca and Hope in the passageway.

"What are you doing here?" demanded the officer.

Rebecca ushered Hope behind her. "We live here," she seethed, hands on her hips in defiance. "What are *you* doing here?"

Rebecca's fire caught the officer off guard and he fumbled his response. "Well, why, what…W-why haven't you left?" he blurted.

"My mother is too sick to move," Rebecca said matter-of-factly. "And as we are no threat to you, we thought we'd be safe." She narrowed her eyes. "For even the British wouldn't harm innocents, surely."

Just then General Arnold entered the tavern. "What have we here, Lieutenant?"

"This girl says her mother is sick in the back room."

Arnold looked sternly at Rebecca and Hope. "Where is your father?" he asked.

"Away, likely fighting *your* men," Rebecca sneered. She felt a slight pressure on her left foot and noticed Hope had stepped on it. A warning, a plea.

Arnold arched his brows at the sisters. "Who else is here?" he asked, head swiveling around the room.

"Doctor Galt."

Arnold's brows rose higher.

"Our mother is sick. He is helping to care for her. As doctors do," Rebecca said pointedly.

Arnold's eyes narrowed to slits. He had been impressed by the girl's gall at first, but now he was starting to find it irritating. "Anyone else?"

"Just our people," Hope said quickly, referring to the Anderson's eight enslaved people who helped operate the tavern. She didn't want to mention the wounded soldier with the doctor.

Rebecca sensed that Arnold was about to send a man to check, however, so she added, “And there is a poor man who lost his arm in battle against *your* men.”

Arnold flinched at the charge, but nodded to the lieutenant to go and see. He looked around the room once more, suddenly realizing it was a tavern. His lips curled in a smile. “Summon your servants,” he said, eyes sharp on Rebecca. “I wish to take dinner here.”

“W-we haven’t much to offer,” said Hope, hoping Arnold would leave.

Arnold ignored her. “Go to the kitchen and see what they have, Sergeant,” he said with a wave of his hand. He then strode into the dining room, motioning for the sisters to follow him.

Rebecca took Hope by the hand and led her into the room. Hope’s hand was cold, clammy. Rebecca squeezed it gently.

The three stood in the dining room, Rebecca near the wall, with Hope still slightly behind her. Arnold had positioned himself in the center of the room, his eyes fixed on Rebecca. “What is your name?” he asked.

"Rebecca Anderson," she replied without the customary curtsey. "And this is my sister, Hope. Who, may I ask, are *you*?"

Arnold grinned like a cat and gave a bow. "General Benedict Arnold, at your service."

It was clear he expected some sort of recognition from the girls, but both stood expressionless—utterly unimpressed that America's most notorious traitor was standing in their dining room.

"And why have you come here?" Rebecca asked curtly.

"To catch that rascal Jefferson, of course," he scoffed, referring to Virginia's governor, Thomas Jefferson.

Rebecca smiled. "I'm afraid you'll be disappointed on that count, he's far away from here by now."

Arnold rubbed his chin. "We'll see, we'll see."

Suddenly, the British lieutenant returned with Doctor Galt. "What she said is true, sir. There's a sick woman and a man without an arm in the back."

"I just took the man's arm," explained Doctor Galt.

"How is the woman?" asked Arnold curtly.

Doctor Galt looked at the sisters, hesitant to reply in front of Hope. He fixed his gaze to the floor. "I'm afraid she is very ill."

"Is there anything I can provide to help?" asked Arnold—to the surprise of Rebecca, Hope, and Doctor Galt.

"Thank you, sir, but she is in God's hands now," Doctor Galt said quietly.

"And the soldier who lost his arm?" continued Arnold.

"He is resting. He lost a lot of blood. Quiet would do them both good."

Arnold nodded. "Well then, doctor, if neither needs your immediate attention, would you be so kind as to look after several captured rebels?" he asked.

"Of course," Doctor Galt replied. "Let me get my bag."

"Lieutenant, take the doctor to the wounded prisoners," instructed General Arnold. "Then tell Colonel Simcoe and Dundas that we shall dine here."

Rebecca listened intently to this exchange, worried that one of the wounded men was James or her father. But she concealed her concern from Arnold.

The sergeant returned from the kitchen to report that although there was nothing prepared for dinner, there was plenty of food available to make a fine meal.

Arnold turned his attention back to Rebecca. “Go tell your cook to prepare dinner for five.” He turned back to the lieutenant. “Accompany her and select the dishes. Make sure there is plenty of ham. I’m fond of Virginia’s ham.”

Rebecca led Hope out of the dining room and to the kitchen, escorted by the lieutenant. It was in a separate building twenty paces from the tavern and Sally, the cook, stood nervously next to the fire. “We need dinner for five, Sally,” Rebecca said. “Make sure there is plenty of ham.” She glanced at the lieutenant who nodded his approval.

Just then Sarah, another of the Anderson’s enslaved servants, entered the kitchen with a smile. “Miss Rebecca, Miss Hope, your mother is awake,” she said.

The sisters burst into smiles and dashed out the door, oblivious to the lieutenant who, to his credit, made no effort to stop them.

They returned to the tavern, entered their mother’s room quietly, and went to her bed. Mrs. Anderson was very weak, but awake, and she smiled at her daughters.

"Go back and tell Sally to warm up the broth," Rebecca instructed Sarah. She then reached for a pitcher of water and poured it in a glass, passing the glass to Hope.

"Here, Mother, drink," Hope said softly as she offered her the glass. "Doctor Galt says you must drink and rest."

Mrs. Anderson raised her head from the pillow and Rebecca cradled it with her arm to hold her up. Their mother took the glass and sipped some water, then smiled weakly and laid back down, handing the glass to Rebecca as she did so. Hope stepped forward and hugged her mother while Rebecca felt her forehead. "I think your fever has broken," Rebecca grinned.

Mrs. Anderson did not smile back. Worry was etched all over her face instead. "Where is your father?" she asked, completely unaware of what had occurred over the past few days.

"He's away, Mother," Rebecca replied gently. "But he'll be back soon."

"How long have I been sick?"

"Not long," Hope said quickly, not wanting to worry her.

Sarah returned with a bowl of broth and passed it to Rebecca. "Here, eat this to keep up your strength."

Mrs. Anderson sat up in bed and Rebecca fed her the broth. Finally, Mrs. Anderson smiled. "I have such wonderful daughters. I have always been so proud of you girls." Both sisters blushed in response.

Mrs. Anderson finished her broth and laid back down with a sigh of exertion. "You must get more rest," Rebecca told her as she fluffed the pillow.

"Yes, yes," Mrs. Anderson replied, suddenly feeling light headed. "Wake me though, when your father returns."

"I will," Rebecca promised, relieved that she didn't have to mention the soldier sleeping on the other side of the room—or the British troops inside the tavern. "You just rest some more, Mother." Rebecca caressed her mother's forehead and hair until she fell back to sleep.

"Stay with her, Sarah," whispered Rebecca, then she crossed the room to check on the sleeping soldier. He seemed fine; blissfully oblivious to the world around him and all its happenings.

Poor lad, thought Rebecca as she grimaced at his bandaged arm, amputated at the elbow. *Poor lad.*

Rebecca and Hope exited the room. "Is Momma going to be alright?" Hope whispered.

Rebecca patted her sister's shoulder. *She must be so worried,* she thought. "I think so," she smiled gently. "She seems much improved."

"What about Father?"

"Oh, I'm sure he is fine as well," Rebecca said, waving her hand in dismissal. "He'll be back soon."

"How long are," Hope's eyes darted around, her voice dropped even lower, "*these* people going to stay?"

Rebecca bit her lip. "I don't know," she said. "Hopefully not long."

Just then two officers entered the tavern. "Where is General Arnold?" one asked tersely.

"He's in there," Rebecca answered, pointing to the dining room just a few steps away.

The officers entered the room and bowed to Arnold, who stood and returned the courtesy. Rebecca had moved to follow them but stopped in the doorway, peering nervously into the dining room.

"Gentlemen, sit. Dinner will be served shortly." Arnold gestured for Rebecca to step forward and she complied, leaving Hope in the hallway behind her. Arnold leaned toward Rebecca and whispered, "Be a good girl and see to dinner."

Rebecca grimaced and left the room. "Go and see to Mother," she said to Hope, wanting to put as much distance as possible between her sister and Arnold and his men. "But don't wake her if she is sleeping."

Hope heeded her sister's request and disappeared into their mother's room. Rebecca then went to the kitchen to check on dinner.

Ben was in the kitchen waiting to bring the dishes to the officers. Rebecca walked up to him, her voice barely audible as she leaned in close. "I want you to listen carefully to what they say at dinner," she said. "But don't be obvious—act like you always act when you wait table."

Ben, who was in his late twenties, stared intently at Rebecca, eyes wide with concern. He was well aware of the risk she was asking him to take, and wasn't sure he wanted to take it. There was a long pause. Ben swallowed hard and then nodded in agreement.

"I'll be in there as well," continued Rebecca. "But I suspect they'll be careful about what they say around me." Her eyes hardened as they met Ben's. "Neither one of us can get caught listening though, so be careful."

Ben nodded once more, then picked up a platter with ham surrounded by cooked peas and onions to take into the dining room.

"I'll serve their drinks," Rebecca called after him. She followed Ben back into the tavern and went to the bar to fetch a bottle of rum.

When she entered the dining room, General Arnold and his officers were congratulating themselves on their victory over the militia. But as soon as they spotted Rebecca they stopped talking. Rebecca smiled at them and placed the bottle of rum on the table.

"Forgive me, sirs," she said. "But given the cold I assumed some rum would be desired."

The officers beamed in agreement and Colonel Simcoe reached for the bottle.

"Would you like anything else to drink?" Rebecca asked, her eyes focused on Arnold.

"Some cider and wine," Arnold replied. "Port, if you have it."

Rebecca retreated back to the bar and waited several minutes. She wanted the officers to indulge in the rum to loosen their tongues. Finally, she drew a pitcher of cider from a barrel behind the bar—but filled it only half way.

If I bring a full pitcher, they'll tell me to leave it, she thought. She needed a reason to keep coming and going into the room.

Her ploy had worked with the cider, but later when she returned with a bottle of wine to pour, and then attempted to leave with it, General Arnold grabbed her by the arm. "Leave the bottle," he murmured, his voice like gravel. "And bring another."

Rebecca forced her arm from his grip, hoping he did not notice her shaking. "Yes, sir," she said as she turned to leave. *He knows,* she thought, a cool sweat breaking over her forehead.

After a few steadying breaths, Rebecca returned—reluctantly—with another bottle of wine. Ben had brought the rest of the food, and the officers were now focused on eating. Rebecca set the bottle on a side table behind General Arnold and then stood nearby, seemingly unnoticed, ready and waiting to pour another glass.

The rum, cider and wine had indeed loosened the officers' tongues—just as she'd hoped.

"I want you to join Ewald at the foundry," Arnold said to Colonel Simcoe, referring to one of the few foundries in

Virginia that made cannons. It was upriver a few miles in Westham. "Take what you can there and burn the rest."

"I shall march as soon as I finish here," Simcoe replied.

Arnold turned to Colonel Dundas. "Your men are to stay watchful in town," he said. "We've likely stirred a hornet's nest."

Rebecca noticed that their wine glasses were empty so she poured another glass for each, then left the room, trying to give the impression she cared little for what they discussed.

She remained, however, just outside the door, and could still hear the officers—whose volume had increased due to the influence of alcohol—clearly.

"I want your men back by midnight, Colonel," Arnold said. "We need to leave tomorrow, before we're cut off."

"Damn that storm," Colonel Dundas grumbled. "What rotten luck. Those men would have been useful here."

Rebecca did not know the context of Dundas's comments, but he was referring to four hundred missing soldiers whose transport ships had been blown off course during their voyage to Virginia from New York.

Colonel Simcoe rose suddenly from the table, the sound of the chair scratching against the floor startling Rebecca. What if she was caught eavesdropping?

"I must be off," the colonel said as Rebecca scurried back to the bar to grab another bottle of wine.

She passed Colonel Simcoe in the hallway. He stared down at the bottle and then drawled over his shoulder, "Careful, gentlemen. I do believe she is trying to get you drunk."

Simcoe's comment had been said lightly, with a slight chuckle in his voice, but when Rebecca entered the room, Arnold waved off the new bottle. "We've had enough," he said firmly.

Colonel Dundas rose to leave, and General Arnold asked him to send in Lieutenant Graves. "I intend to stay here tonight," Arnold said, his eyes searching for Rebecca. They glimmered when they found her. "See that two rooms are prepared," he said.

Rebecca's stomach clenched, but she nodded and left the room. When she returned a few minutes later, General Arnold and the others were gone. Ten English shillings were left on the table as payment for dinner.

Rebecca was hesitant to accept the money, but ultimately did so, figuring her father could decide whether to keep it or not. She then went to check on her mother.

Mrs. Anderson was still sleeping soundly. Hope laid on a blanket on the floor beside her, face peaceful in sleep. Rebecca heaved a sigh of relief and then ventured to the kitchen to find Ben.

"Did you hear anything?" Rebecca asked.

"Not really, Miss Rebecca," replied Ben regretfully. "But they did seem worried about being trapped here."

"Did you hear any numbers mentioned?" Rebecca pressed.

Ben thought for a moment, trying to recall. "Why yes," he said with a start. "One of 'em said four hundred. But four hundred of what, I didn't hear."

Rebecca paused, wracking her brain for any connection. She knew Arnold was missing men—perhaps the four hundred referred to them? She wasn't sure how many men were in Richmond, or how many were left at Westover, but it seemed to her that Arnold's force was far too small to stay very long in Richmond. Militia from all over the state were likely marching to the capital to confront him.

That must be what he meant by stirring a hornet's nest, she thought. *They really are afraid the militia will trap them here.*

Rebecca told Ben to find Sarah. "Tell her to prepare all the rooms upstairs."

General Arnold had gone next door to the courthouse to meet with a number of Richmond merchants who had been summoned while he'd dined. Arnold had a proposition for them: if they delivered their barrels of tobacco, wine, rum, sail cloth, and bolts of fabric that were in town and aboard merchant ships anchored in the river, he would pay them half their value. If they did not deliver the items, however, Arnold would seize what he could and burn the rest.

The merchants had been tempted by the offer. After all, half value was better than nothing. So, they reached out to Governor Jefferson—who was across the river in Manchester—asking for permission to accept Arnold's offer. Jefferson received the request in the evening and immediately refused it, calling the arrangement ransom. Arnold would not learn of Jefferson's reaction until the next morning, however.

Arnold remained at the courthouse tending to his army until 9 p.m. before finally retiring to the tavern.

"Are my rooms ready?" he asked Rebecca when he entered.

"They are," she replied coldly, the flame of the candle she held flickering with the cool breeze.

"Good," Arnold said. "And how many rooms are upstairs?"

"Four."

"Have a fire started in the two. And send a plate of ham, some bread, cheese, and a bottle of port to my room." He took the candle from Rebecca and walked upstairs.

"Such entitlement," Rebecca fumed under her breath. But she did as she was told, stalking carefully in the dark to the kitchen to replace the candle that had been stolen from her, and the items Arnold had requested. She set the items on the floor next to Arnold's closed door and knocked, then turned on her heel and hurried downstairs. She had had enough of the infamous traitor for one day.

Arnold, however, wasn't finished with Rebecca. "Have some more wood brought up," he called down the stairs before she'd reached the bottom. "For all the rooms."

Rebecca told Ben to get Ned, an enslaved lad of fourteen, to bring the firewood. She then went to her mother's room, threw some wood on the fire there, and checked on her mother, who smiled briefly at Rebecca, still half in a dream, before drifting back to sleep.

The soldier who had lost his arm had been moved from the tavern hours before by the British, so Rebecca scooped Hope up from the floor and placed her on the empty bed. When Hope had settled, Rebecca squeezed in next to her, careful not to wake her.

She yawned once, her eyes closing against her will. Her last thought was the realization that she didn't know whether James or her father were even safe. She'd been too busy to fret about it, and now she was too tired to worry. *They'll be alright,* she thought. *They have to be alright.*

James and Major Anderson were indeed safe. They were a few miles north of Richmond with a small force of militia, waiting for reinforcements.

Their thoughts mirrored Rebecca's—both consumed with worry about their loved ones.

"Let them be alright, Lord," prayed James that night. "Please let them be alright."

Chapter Four

The Cost of War

Sometime after midnight, Rebecca was awakened by the arrival of Colonel Simcoe and Captain Ewald. They had completed their mission at Westham.

"It is destroyed," Rebecca heard Simcoe report to Arnold, who was standing at the top of the stairs to receive their report.

"Excellent, gentlemen," said Arnold, and Rebecca could easily picture his sly, snake-like smile. "There are two rooms available here for you, if you so desire," he added.

Colonel Simcoe accepted the offer, but Captain Ewald—who fiercely disliked Arnold—waved the general off, saying he must see to his men.

"Very well, Captain," replied Arnold. "Very well."
He returned to his room, abruptly shutting the door. Rebecca willed herself to stay awake, unsure if any other conversation would occur. But after a few minutes of heavy silence, she allowed sleep to take her.

The next morning, during breakfast, General Arnold received Jefferson's rejection. "Bloody fool," he growled, crumpling it in his hands. "Lieutenant Wilson, find Captain Robinson and tell him to secure as many vessels in the river as he can. Concentrate on those carrying tobacco," he barked.

Colonel Dundas, who had taken one of the rooms upstairs, was also at the table. Arnold instructed him to burn the warehouses and public buildings. "We leave by noon," he snapped, fingers still tensing over Jefferson's ruined rejection.

Rebecca had just entered the dining room when Arnold gave the order. One hand flew to her chest, the other clamped over her mouth. "You're going to burn the town?" she gasped in disbelief.

Arnold huffed a laugh. "Blame your governor for being unreasonable," he said simply, rising from the table. "It won't be the whole town," he added, as if that made the news easier to hear, "just the public buildings and anything of value you Virginians can use for the war." He gave Rebecca a wolfish grin and then left the room.

Rebecca rushed to her mother's room, unsure what to do. Her mother was still too weak to resume her duties as the mistress of the house, but she had passed the worst of her illness and was recovering well. Still, Rebecca doubted she was well enough to be moved if they needed to escape.

"Rebecca," her mother called. "What's wrong? You're pale as a ghost. I heard quite a commotion, is everything alright?"

"Yes," Rebecca lied, not wishing to upset her mother. "Everything is fine." *Even if I tell her the truth,* she thought, *what can be done? We are helpless against them.*

About two hours later, Rebecca heard shouting outside the tavern. She rushed to the front door and gasped at the sight of the courthouse ablaze—torched, per Arnold's order.

Several soldiers were pointing frantically toward the sky, prompting Rebecca to step into the street to get a better look. Embers from the courthouse blaze had ignited the tavern's roof!

"Mother! Hope!" she cried as she raced back inside. "Fire! Fire! The tavern's on fire!" she yelled to anyone who could hear as she burst through the front door. Ben and Ned scrambled to her from two directions. "Is anyone upstairs? Where's Sarah and Jane?" Rebecca asked frantically.

"Everyone's out back washing laundry," Ben replied.

From the corner of her eye, Rebecca saw Hope emerge from their mother's room, her eyes wide with fright.

"We need to get Mother," Rebecca said calmly as she walked toward Hope. "Can you do that?"

Hope nodded and went back into the room. Rebecca turned back to face Ned and Ben, motioning them to follow her. "Grab the trunks," she directed as they all entered the bedchamber.

Hope was at the side of their mother's bed, a hand on her shoulder. Mrs. Anderson asked, "What is it, dear? What's the matter?" as she struggled to rise from the bed.

Rebecca willed her voice to steady. "We have to go, Mother. We haven't time to dress properly. The tavern is on fire and we have to go *now.*"

Mrs. Anderson bolted upright, her hands grasping the sheets tightly. "Help her with her shoes," Rebecca told Hope as she grabbed her mother's cloak and wrapped it around her.

The sisters helped Mrs. Anderson rise to her feet. "Hold her steady," Rebecca said as she let go to gather up the sheets and blankets from the bed. "We'll need these." She handed the bundle of bedding to her mother. Rebecca then ducked under her mother's arm; Hope did the same on her other side and they guided Mrs. Anderson out of the tavern.

The roof was fully engulfed by the time they reached the street, flames roaring into the sky, but Rebecca felt that more could be saved from the house—furniture was not easily come by, especially after six years of war, and if they lost their belongings… Rebecca grimaced at the thought. Thankfully, Ben and Ned, joined by Will, the Anderson's enslaved stable hand, had already ventured back inside to retrieve more things.

The fire was growing in intensity, and Rebecca realized there was little time to save what they could. "Won't you help them?" she pleaded to a group of British soldiers who were just standing and watching the fire. One of them scoffed at her, but after a moment three soldiers handed their muskets and cartridge boxes to their comrades and dashed into the house.

"You're bloody fools," yelled the one who had scoffed. Rebecca narrowed her eyes at him.

The soldiers re-emerged a minute later, behind Ben and Ned, who were carrying Mr. Anderson's desk out of the tavern. The soldiers had gathered up some Windsor chairs. Will followed after them with a gaming table. He struggled with it by himself and placed it in the street.

"Come on you cowards," one of the soldiers growled. "There's still more to come out."

Not keen on having been called cowards, two other British solders joined the effort. More chairs and tables, along with two punch bowls, were all saved from the flames and placed in a pile in the street with the other items.

Rebecca ushered her mother and sister further away from the tavern, from the flames. They had moved just in time, for suddenly the windows shattered—unable to withstand the heat—scattering glass everywhere. "Shield your eyes," Rebecca shouted, but her voice was lost amongst a great groan. The tavern's roof was buckling. Rebecca stood frozen in terror as she watched the roof collapse into the building. *Nothing else can be saved,* she realized. *It's too dangerous.*

General Arnold suddenly appeared before the Andersons. "I am sorry for your loss, madam," he said stiffly. "It was not my intention to harm your property."

Rebecca glared at Arnold. Intention or not, his actions had brought ruin to her family—and undoubtedly many other inhabitants of Richmond. She hadn't noticed it at first, but all around them plumes of smoke from other fires rose in the sky.

"You've ruined people's lives," Rebecca said callously.

Arnold winced at the statement, but then heaved a great sigh. "The cost of war, madam. The cost of war."

Miraculously, the fire had not spread to the kitchen and other out buildings of the Anderson property. Not everyone was as lucky as the Andersons, however.

Arnold's cost of war included nearly all of Richmond's public buildings, several private businesses and warehouses, and many other private homes. As Arnold had said, it was not his intention to torch anything other than Richmond's public buildings and warehouses. But fire was not easily controlled.

As the fire reached its zenith and the second floor of the tavern collapsed, all of the Anderson's enslaved people gathered around Mrs. Anderson in the street, offering words of comfort. Several had lost their own personal possessions in the fire as well, yet they mourned for Mrs. Anderson's loss. Rebecca was touched by their concern. *I must find someplace for all of us to go,* she resolved.

“Now that you’ve left us without a home,” she snarled at Arnold, “the least you could do is watch our possessions while I search for a place to stay.”

Arnold flinched at her words, but then nodded slightly in agreement. He ordered a sergeant and two men to remain with the Anderson’s property. Ben, Ned, and Will stayed too; they kept their distance and watched the soldiers guard the possessions. The others, Sarah, Jane, and Sally, along with her two children, Nancy and Polly, followed Rebecca up the street. Mrs. Anderson leaned on Sally and Sarah for support. Hope walked alongside Rebecca, who led the procession. Rebecca took Hope’s hand and squeezed it tightly, as if to say everything would be alright.

They made their way to the Buchanan’s residence, just several lots away. Mrs. Buchanan had witnessed the entire incident with her children from their porch. As soon as she glimpsed the Andersons, she rushed toward them, arms waving. “Come dear, come in from the cold,” Mrs. Buchanan urged, much to Rebecca’s relief.

“Thank you,” Rebecca said. “Truly thank you.”

They all followed Mrs. Buchanan inside. She instructed Sally and Sarah to take Mrs. Anderson upstairs.

“Use the second bedroom on the left,” she called up to them as they climbed the stairs. Rebecca and Hope followed them and helped their mother into bed.

Mrs. Anderson was exhausted by the effort and quickly fell asleep. “I will stay with her,” declared Sarah. Rebecca smiled and patted Sarah’s hand in thanks. She led Hope and Sally back downstairs, where Mrs. Buchanan was waiting for them.

“Betty, take Mrs. Anderson’s people to the kitchen and see that they get something to eat,” said Mrs. Buchanan to her enslaved woman. Rebecca smiled in thanks.

A wave of relief swept over Rebecca, followed by one of exhaustion, but she pushed it aside.

“Thank you for your kindness, Mrs. Buchanan. Can I impose on you just a bit more and ask that you watch after Hope? I need to return to the tavern.”

“My dear,” Mrs. Buchanan gasped, eyes wide with shock, “do you think you should?”

Rebecca nodded. “I must,” she said firmly.

Rebecca returned to the tavern and found General Arnold mounted upon his horse, about to ride off. “General Arnold, sir!” she yelled, determined to talk to him before he departed. “General Arnold!”

He turned his head then whirled his horse around. His eyes hardened as he stared down at Rebecca. “Yes?”

Rebecca seethed with anger, but knew she needed his help, so she took several deep breaths and held her tongue. “Sir, can your troops help us move our possessions to our stable? They cannot remain here in the street, it isn’t safe.”

Arnold stared at Rebecca for a moment, then said to a lieutenant standing nearby, “See to it, Lieutenant.”

Rebecca was most concerned about her father’s desk, which she knew he valued immensely. She followed the soldiers who carried the desk and had them place it deep in the stable.

The rest of the salvaged items—chairs, tables, trunks of clothing, several punch bowls, and a few other miscellaneous things—were also placed in the stable.

The soldiers left and Rebecca sent Ben, Ned, and Will, who had all helped move the possessions, to Mrs. Buchanan’s kitchen to join the others and get something to eat. “I’ll be along shortly,” she said to Ben, who was hesitant to leave Rebecca alone.

When Ben finally departed, Rebecca made her way to the kitchen to inspect it for damage. She had not seen flames wrap themselves around the structure, but you never knew with fire. Thankfully, the kitchen truly had been spared, and Rebecca heaved a sigh of relief as she surveyed it. *Sarah and Jane can stay here with Sally and the girls,* she thought. *But what of Ben, Ned, and Will?* Each slept in the tavern upon mats on the floor during the winter, and early January was certainly the coldest of the colder months.

Rebecca left the kitchen and headed back to Mrs. Buchanan's. Smoke still billowed from the ruins of the tavern, which was now little more than a heap of debris, but the flames had died down. Rebecca could tell there was nothing more to be salvaged, and she worried how her father would react. *He's worked so hard; this will devastate him.*

At noon, General Arnold formed his troops and commenced a march back to Westover. Much of Richmond smoldered in their wake.

Major Anderson and James arrived back in Richmond late in the afternoon. They were both shocked at the loss of the tavern, but relieved when they learned that everyone had escaped unharmed and were with Mrs. Buchanan.

Dinner had ended an hour earlier at Mrs. Buchanan's, but everyone, including Mrs. Anderson, who had gingerly come downstairs on her own when she heard her husband enter the house, gathered around the table to join Major Anderson and James as they had their first meal of the day.

"Thank you, Mrs. Buchanan, for taking our family in," Major Anderson said.

"Of course," Mrs. Buchanan replied. "You can stay as long as you need."

Major Anderson smiled, but shook his head. "James and I can't stay long, unfortunately. There's talk of striking the enemy on their march back to Westover." He paused, glancing around the room before he continued. "And we all can't possibly stay here. It would be too much of a burden on you."

"What about your brother?" Mrs. Anderson suggested, referring to her husband's brother, James, who had moved his armory from Williamsburg to Richmond. "Can't we stay with him?"

Major Anderson shook his head again. "I'm afraid not," he said sadly. "They burned his forge and house, too."

"I know we all can't stay in the kitchen, but it survived the fire unscathed, and perhaps Sarah and Jane can stay there with Sally and her girls," Rebecca suggested.

"That's a fine idea," replied her father with a smile and nod.

"But what of the others?" asked Hope, referring to the enslaved men of the Anderson household. "And what of us?"

Mrs. Buchanan, who had been sitting on a solution all along but was hesitant to interject, finally spoke up. "They can stay on our plantation just outside of town," she announced. "And you and your family can stay here as long as you need."

Major Anderson appreciated the offer and accepted the invitation for his family to stay, but had another idea for his three enslaved men. "I think I want them to remain on the property," said Major Anderson. "We'll put them in the laundry house for the time being. It won't be very comfortable, but they can keep warm by a fire. Might we borrow some mats and bedding for them to sleep on?"

"Certainly, certainly," replied Mrs. Buchanan.

With the immediate crisis resolved, Major Anderson and James rose from the table. "Thank you again, Mrs. Buchanan. But we must return to the army," he announced. "Maybe we can repay the traitor for what he's done here."

As they all walked toward the door, Rebecca reached for her father and took his arm.

"He's missing men," Rebecca told him. "Arnold's missing men. Ben heard four hundred. And I heard him say they were to return to Portsmouth."

Major Anderson drew back, surprised. The information itself didn't surprise him, but rather that fact that his daughter had somehow obtained it.

"Did he say why the men are missing?" he asked.

"A storm blew them astray, I think."

"Hmmm," her father mused. "That means that unless they sank, which we can only hope they did, those missing men will likely join him soon." Major Anderson turned to James. "How many men do you think they had today?"

"No more than a thousand," replied James. "Likely less."

"And they must have left some at Westover. So, all told, there's probably less than fifteen hundred troops with Arnold. General Nelson may have that many raised by now, and General Steuben nearly as many. We might be able to crush him at Westover before he leaves," Major Anderson said excitedly.

"I'm long overdue to join General Nelson," James reminded him. "Let us ride for Williamsburg. Surely he is there, or even past there, by now."

Major Anderson agreed. He thanked Mrs. Buchanan once again for her kindness and hospitality, hugged and kissed Rebecca and Hope, then led his wife aside to say goodbye.

James turned to Rebecca. "I don't know when I'll see you again, Becca. I've got to return to General Nelson, and if Arnold stays in Virginia, it may be a while before I can get back."

Rebecca gave him a tight smile. She hated to say goodbye, but understood James had a duty to fulfill. "You just take care of yourself, James Southall," she said, placing both hands on his shoulders. "We'll be fine here." The two embraced one last time, and then Major Anderson and James departed.

Chapter Five

Will the Militia Fight?

James and Major Anderson rode east, in the direction of Westover, just as it began to rain hard. *If only it had rained like this earlier,* thought James, remembering the charred remains of the Anderson's tavern. The pair made slow progress in the rain and about three hours into their journey, were startled by a party of horsemen who had been hiding among some trees on a curve in the road.

"Where are *you* off to?" demanded a voice that emerged from the shadows. James could see the men were militia and immediately relaxed.

"I'm Major Anderson of Richmond, and this is Lieutenant Southall," responded the major. "Who are you with?"

"General Nelson posted us here," replied a different voice, his face still in shadow. The soldier who had stopped them turned sharply in the saddle and glared at the soldier for speaking out of turn. He looked to be a sergeant with the militia, and apparently commanded the small party.

"Nelson? Is he close by?" asked James excitedly.

The sergeant eyed James suspiciously, not certain he and Major Anderson could be trusted. "He's near enough."

"Can you take us to him?" asked Major Anderson.

"I cannot," replied the sergeant. "My orders are to guard this road."

"Lieutenant Southall is General Nelson's aide, and I have information for him about the enemy. We've come from Richmond. It's vital that we see him," insisted Major Anderson.

The sergeant squinted at Major Anderson, lost in thought for a moment, before finally concluding he was telling the truth. "I'm Sergeant Pleasants," he said. "I'll send loud mouth there," referring to the soldier who had spoken out of turn, "with you to find General Nelson."

The three rode southeast for two hours in the pouring rain, crossing the Chickahominy at Long Bridge, and continued to Holt's Forge. They found General Nelson in a tavern still awake.

"Major Anderson, you've brought my missing aide," Nelson declared when they entered the tavern. "Is the rain letting up?"

"It has not, sir," replied the major. "It's a difficult night for anyone who may be out in it."

Nelson frowned. Most of his poorly armed men—just four hundred strong—were sheltering in hastily built brush huts that did little to stop the unrelenting rain. Nelson's one comfort was that General Arnold and his troops were likely exposed to the rain as well.

Major Anderson shared the information that Rebecca had delivered in Richmond; General Nelson's eyes sparkling as he listened. "If only I had more men and more arms," he muttered when Major Anderson had finished. "We might strike him before he reached Westover."

James stepped closer to the general and asked, "How may I be of service, sir?"

Nelson looked at James. "Place your belongings in the corner. You and Major Anderson will sleep here tonight." He turned to an officer standing off in the corner. "Lieutenant Peyton," he said, "have someone tend to their horses. We shall move closer to the enemy tomorrow."

General Nelson announced that there was little else to do until the morning, and instructed the officers to turn in. "I have one dispatch to write before I turn in myself," said the general. "Hopefully this blasted rain will let up by morning." He then bid the two good night and headed for his bedchamber, candle in hand.

James and Major Anderson shared a room upstairs in the tavern with two other officers. Since the bed was already occupied, each slept on a stuffed tick on the floor. They joined General Nelson for breakfast in the morning.

"There is little we can do, gentlemen," declared General Nelson, "until more militia arrive with ammunition. The rain last night ruined much of the men's powder. We shall remain here until reinforcements arrive."

"Sir," Major Anderson started, "with your permission, I would like to return to Richmond to attend to my family. I have no troops to command here, and the enemy burned my tavern yesterday."

General Nelson's eyes flickered with something that looked like pity. "Of course, Major," he said. "I am sorry for your loss. Was anyone harmed?"

"All escaped injury, sir," replied Major Anderson.

General Nelson glanced at James, aware of his relationship with Anderson's oldest daughter. "I'm glad to hear it, but am sorry for the loss of your property."

Major Anderson left James with General Nelson after breakfast and reached Richmond by mid-afternoon.

Rebecca and Mrs. Buchannan greeted him when he entered the Buchannan's home.

"Because the British burned his forge and house here, Uncle James is going to return to Williamsburg and has invited us to join him," announced Rebecca excitedly. "That is, assuming Arnold hasn't burned his house there, too. It's been unoccupied since last spring."

Major Anderson nodded at the news. *It might be best for them to return to Williamsburg,* he thought, *provided Arnold goes to Portsmouth*—which, Rebecca had claimed, were his intentions.

Major Anderson bowed to Mrs. Buchanan, then leaned forward and kissed his eldest daughter on the cheek. "How are your mother and sister?" he asked.

"They are well, Father. Mother has recovered nicely."

"Take me to them."

Rebecca led him upstairs. "Where's James?" she asked, a bit embarrassed that she hadn't asked sooner.

"He's with General Nelson. We found him last night in Charles City County," replied her father. "A general's aide is a very safe position," he reassured Rebecca.

When they entered the bedroom of Mrs. Anderson, they found her sitting in a chair, sewing. "Don't get up, dear," her husband said as he walked to her and kissed her on the forehead. Hope sprung from the floor and hugged her father around the waist.

"What are we to do, Father?" Hope asked.

"We'll be fine, dear," he said, patting her on the head. "Let me talk to your mother."

Rebecca took Hope by the hand and left the room so her parents could talk in private. Ten minutes later, her parents appeared. "We've decided to accept your uncle's kind invitation and return to Williamsburg to stay with him," said Mrs. Anderson.

"I will need to go there first, to ensure there is still a house to go to," added Major Anderson.

Rebecca beamed at her parents' decision. Williamsburg would place her much closer to James.

It took a week for Mr. Anderson to make the arrangements. During this time, General Arnold and his force left Westover and sailed downriver to Portsmouth. Mr. Anderson returned from Williamsburg and announced the city had been spared from Arnold's wrath.

The Anderson's left Richmond on January 17th, the same day that Rebecca's dear friend and James's younger brother, John Southall, found himself engaged in a bloody battle in South Carolina. It was a battle that would help change the course of the war.

Seventeen-year-old John Southall had always been fascinated by war and had joined the Continental army in the winter of 1780, soon after his 16th birthday. A participant in the disastrous American defeats at Waxhaws and Camden in 1780, John's attitude toward war had changed considerably.

The factors that had first drawn John to join the army— namely, adventure and glory—faded quickly as he learned the reality of army life and war. The Americans had suffered defeat after defeat in South Carolina in 1780, suppressing American morale and support for the war. Still, John refused to give up. A strong sense of duty drove him on.

Having been wounded at Waxhaws in May, John had healed during the summer of 1780, only to then be stricken with smallpox. It was during his recuperation from smallpox in Hillsborough, North Carolina, that John had met Abigail Jenkins, the sixteen-year-old daughter of a widowed doctor. Abigail nursed John through the illness, and in doing so, sparked a friendship that had blossomed into romance.

More than three months had passed since John had last seen Abigail. During that time, he'd served in Captain Andew Wallace's company of Virginia Continentals. They were attached to General Danial Morgan's light infantry corps. This detachment was formed from among the entire Continental force in the south—some fifteen hundred Continental soldiers from Maryland, Delaware, and Virginia. Several hundred militia from Virginia and the Carolinas were also a part of the Southern army.

The difference between Continental and militia soldiers was enormous. Continentals were full time soldiers who served in the army for several years, while militia were civilians called into the field for short periods during an emergency. Most militia proved unreliable in battle—as had been the case at Camden a few months earlier, when nearly two thousand of them had fled without firing a single shot.

General Morgan's light corps consisted of three hundred of the best Continental troops in the army. John was one of them. They had been posted near the border of North and South Carolina back in late October, shielding the main army—which was in Charlotte, North Carolina—from the British in South Carolina.

In late December, the American commander of the Southern Army, General Nathanael Greene of Rhode Island, had sent General Morgan and his detachment southwestward into South Carolina's backcountry.

Greene had marched the rest of the army eastward to find a more reliable source of food for his hungry troops and horses. The winter weather was harsh, so the British army under General Charles Cornwallis had been content to remain in Winnsboro, in the middle of South Carolina, awaiting spring and its milder weather before retaking the field.

It was always a challenge to move large armies in the winter because the natural food source for transport animals—specifically, grass—disappeared. Hay and other fodder thus had to be hauled with an army on the march, and this created a huge burden on both the animals and troops. As a result, most armies stockpiled hay and other animal fodder in an encampment for the entirety of the winter season, waiting until the grass returned so their animals could eat off the land while on the march.

General Greene had had little choice, however. There wasn't enough food in Charlotte to feed his army. So, he had sent Morgan with a small force capable of living off the land to the west, while he had marched east with the rest of the army in search of an adequate food supply for the winter.

Morgan's appearance in the backcountry had surprised General Cornwallis. It threatened an important British outpost called Ninety-Six, so he had sent one of his best officers—Colonel Banastre Tarleton—with his British Legion of cavalry and infantry, as well as a battalion of British infantry, to challenge Morgan. Tarleton's British Legion were loyalist Americans who fought for the British side, and they were every bit as good as British Redcoats—as they had more than proven months earlier at Waxhaws.

Tarleton had proposed that he and General Cornwallis move against Morgan in a pincer movement. Tarleton would march straight at Morgan from the south, while Cornwallis would converge on him from the east. If Morgan chose to stand and fight Tarleton, the British commander expected to destroy him like he had done at Waxhaws. And if Morgan retreated and tried to reunite with General Greene, General Cornwallis could cut him off and trap Morgan in a vice. Either way, Tarleton expected to destroy Daniel Morgan and his small force.

Cornwallis had approved the plan in early January and had sent reinforcements to Tarleton, bringing his force to over one thousand men, nearly three hundred of which were cavalry. He also had two cannons, something Morgan lacked. While the British moved to attack Morgan, the American commander, alongside his small force of three hundred Continentals, one hundred twenty cavalry, and a couple hundred militia who had joined him in South Carolina, encamped on the Pacolet River, waiting for more militia reinforcements to arrive. For now, they were unaware of the danger that was approaching.

John Southall was proud to be a part of Morgan's Light Corps. General Morgan was famous throughout America for his earlier exploits in Canada and Saratoga. But John was growing restless of their situation on the Pacolet. Low on numbers and food, they just sat there day after day, waiting and waiting for reinforcements. John used the time to write to Abigail in Hillsborough.

January 8, 1781

Dearest Abby,

We remain encamped on a river in the backcountry of South Carolina, waiting for the people of this state and Georgia to join us. Thus far we have been disappointed, which might actually be a blessing because we barely have enough food to feed *ourselves.*

We number around six hundred men, more Continentals than militia, thank God! General Morgan seems very annoyed at the situation, and the talk in camp is that he wants to march to Georgia, but he is awaiting permission from General Greene.

The men with me in Captain Wallace's company are good soldiers, and I have made a number of friends. Although I am still younger than most of them, my service at Waxhaws and Camden is known to all, and there is a degree of respect shown to me as a result.

I know not what to expect, Abby, but doubt we can remain here much longer. I would hope that we might return to Hillsborough, but that would leave the enemy free reign of South Carolina. Even worse, they would likely follow us, and then we would bring the enemy to you.

I hope you and your father are safe and well. I will write again when there is something new to tell you. Until then, I remain,

Your Most Affectionate Friend,

John

Another week passed before startling news arrived in camp. The British were moving against them. Reports of both Tarleton's and Cornwallis's movements had alerted General Morgan to the danger. He surprised the British in response. He withdrew northwestward, away from General Greene—not northeastward, as the British had expected. This took him further away from Cornwallis, but not Tarleton, who was rapidly pursuing Morgan from the south. A sense of urgency swept through Morgan's troops as they marched.

"Where do you think we're going?" John asked Sergeant Collins, his platoon sergeant, as they marched.

"I don't know," replied the sergeant, "but it ain't Georgia."

Morgan was eager to cross the Broad River before Tarleton caught him. He halted just a few miles from the river in an open area known as Cowpens late in the day on

January 16th. There was not enough light left to reach the river and cross it safely, so Morgan decided to camp there.

When General Morgan halted at Cowpens, he did not intend to stand and fight there. The ground was good for camping, but less than ideal for defense. The area was often used by farmers who would stop to let their cattle graze on the way to markets in the east. Relatively flat and open, with scattered woods on both sides of the field, there was no high ground or water obstruction on which to anchor his flanks and prevent Tarleton's cavalry from sweeping around behind them. So, Morgan's plan was to cross the river in the morning and find a stronger piece of ground on which to defend.

It was bitterly cold in mid-January, and John and his comrades huddled around campfires in the early evening.

As they shivered against the wind, a soldier walked up to them and said, "Be on the alert, boys. Ole Morgan is on the prowl."

John looked down the line of campfires and noticed General Morgan and several officers walking from one to the next, pausing for a minute or two before moving on. *What's he up to*? wondered John, as he rubbed his hands to warm them. He nudged the soldier next to him. "Look at that," he whispered.

The soldier looked down the line, then back to John. "That's the militia he's talking to. I wonder why he's spending so much time with them?"

"Probably trying to boost their spirits so they don't run off tonight," John jeered.

Morgan continued to move from campfire to campfire, chatting with the men gathered at each. Eventually, he reached John's group.

"Evening, boys," said the general.

"Evening, sir," came their reply in unison.

"Everyone get enough to eat?" asked General Morgan. There was a chuckle because none of them, including General Morgan, had had a good meal in weeks. Yet they all nodded and answered, "Yes, sir."

Then the soldier next to John asked, "How's the militia doing tonight, General? Think they'll be with us in the morning?"

Morgan gave a small smile and looked directly at the soldier. "They're doing fine, lad. And we're going to need them tomorrow, cause a fight is comin'. Ben Tarleton is itchin' to catch us, and I aim to let him."

John tensed at the mention of Tarleton. He'd had two brushes with him already, and both had ended badly.

"You think the militia will actually stand and fight?" the soldier continued, still unconvinced.

"I do, lad," replied General Morgan. "I've asked them to stand firm and fire a couple of volleys before they withdraw. To thin the redcoat herd. Then I expect you fellas to finish the job."

"We won't let you down, sir," John said earnestly, his eyes fixed on the general.

General Morgan offered him a smile. "I know you won't, son," he said. "I'll tell you what I told them. Just do your duty tomorrow and we'll thrash ole Benny. And then, when you return to your homes, oh how the old folks will bless you and the girls will kiss you for your gallant conduct."

Everyone chuckled at the thought.

"Try to get some rest, boys," Morgan said as he started for the next campfire down the line.

As John and his tentmates squeezed into their tent for the evening, he thought about his previous battles and wondered if his next would be any different. He prayed it would.

Chapter Six

Cowpens

John awoke with a start before sunrise. A flurry of camp activity signaled that something was wrong. The British had stolen a march on Morgan and were just a few miles away. Crossing the river was out of the question now; they'd have to stand and fight at Cowpens.

"Form up, Virginians," called Captain Wallace. "There's work to be done!"

John and the others threw off their blankets and scrambled out of the tent with their muskets and gear. It was still dark and bitterly cold.

"Should we break down the tent?" John asked Sergeant Collins.

"The tents stay up," he replied. "Pack up your personals and leave your packs inside."

The company was formed in a matter of minutes, joined by the Delaware and Maryland Continental companies. John noticed the militia also forming up.

Looks like we've added some since yesterday, he thought.

"Where's the cavalry?" asked a soldier a few spots down the line from John.

"Probably out looking for Benny," replied Sergeant Collins, referring to the British commander, Banastre Tarleton.

Just then Captain Wallace appeared before the company. "The enemy is on their way, boys!" he announced. "And General Morgan has determined to stand and fight here."

John's stomach tightened and his teeth clenched. *So be it then,* he thought.

"Check your muskets, make sure your flints are sharp and tight, and that you have a spare ready if needed," instructed Captain Wallace. "Check your cartridges, too. Make sure none are damaged."

"Take care!" called an officer toward the center of the battalion. "Attention, battalion!"

Everyone snapped to attention and Captain Wallace took his position on the right front of the company, just a few spots away from John, who was also in the front rank.

Lieutenant-Colonel John Eager Howard of Maryland, a veteran of numerous battles in the north and an excellent, brave leader, appeared before the battalion of Continentals, still three hundred strong. General Morgan commanded the entire American force assembled at Cowpens, which had increased to nearly fifteen hundred men with the arrival of additional militia over the evening, but Colonel Howard had direct command of the Continentals.

Next to Colonel Howard stood his aide, Lieutenant Foster, who was issuing the battalion orders on the colonel's behalf. "Prepare to go from line to column… By platoons… To the right wheel… March!"

John and his comrades turned right ninety degrees and formed a long column of platoons.

"To the front… March!"

The column stepped off and marched about half a mile, then turned to the right and halted.

"Prepare to go from column to line… To the left wheel… March!"

The platoons wheeled into position and within seconds, a solid line of Continentals in two ranks was formed, facing south.

"Prime and load!" commanded Colonel Howard to the entire battalion. John reached back and grabbed a musket cartridge from his box. It was a paper tube filled with a musket ball and gunpowder. He ripped the cartridge open with his teeth and poured some of the powder into a pan on the side of the barrel of his musket. He then closed the hammer to keep the powder in place and poured the rest of it, as well as the musket ball—which was still in the paper tube—down the muzzle of the barrel. He withdrew his ramrod and rammed paper and ball down the barrel, then returned his ramrod to its socket and returned his musket to his left shoulder. The whole process, which he had practiced hundreds of times, took only fifteen seconds.

John looked left and noticed a column of militia marching past them, further down the road, and toward the enemy. *That's odd,* he thought. *What's General Morgan up to*?

Others in the line with him had the same thought. "He's not putting the militia up front, is he?" asked one soldier. "They'll never stand."

John couldn't believe it either, but then he remembered what Morgan had said just a few hours earlier.

"They don't have to hold," said John in response. "They just have to fire two volleys to thin the herd."

"*We're* the ones who have to hold," corrected a third soldier.

"Quiet in the ranks!" snapped Sergeant Collins from his position behind Captain Wallace.

John and his comrades were right. Rather than form his troops into one long line of men, which was the customary method of deploying, General Morgan chose a defense in depth.

The Continentals, joined by two battalions of militia, formed Morgan's main line. They were approximately six hundred strong, and positioned to the right of the road on a slight rise of ground. One hundred and fifty yards in front of them, Morgan deployed the rest of the militia—nearly one thousand strong, thanks to the recent arrival of reinforcements. These were the men that Morgan had spent so much time talking to the night before, boosting their spirits and urging them to fire at least two volleys before they withdrew.

One hundred and fifty of these men, all with rifles, which were much more accurate than the smoothbore muskets most of Morgan's men, including John, carried, were detached from the militia and deployed one hundred and fifty yards in front of them. They were ordered to spread out to form a thin skirmish line facing the enemy, and to use trees and brush for cover. "Aim for the Kingbirds," General Morgan instructed, referring to the British officers.

Neither Morgan's skirmish line or his militia line, who were standing shoulder to shoulder in two ranks like the Continentals, were expected to hold firm and stop the enemy. But if they could fire two or three well aimed shots before withdrawing, they might weaken the enemy enough to give the Continentals a chance to finish them off. It seemed like a good plan…in theory.

John and his comrades were not aware of Morgan's entire plan, however. They worried that using the militia up front would lead to disaster. John's mind raced back to what had happened at Camden just five months earlier, when most of the militia had fled without firing a shot. *You can't count on militia,* John worried. *They'll run every time.*

Battle of Cowpens

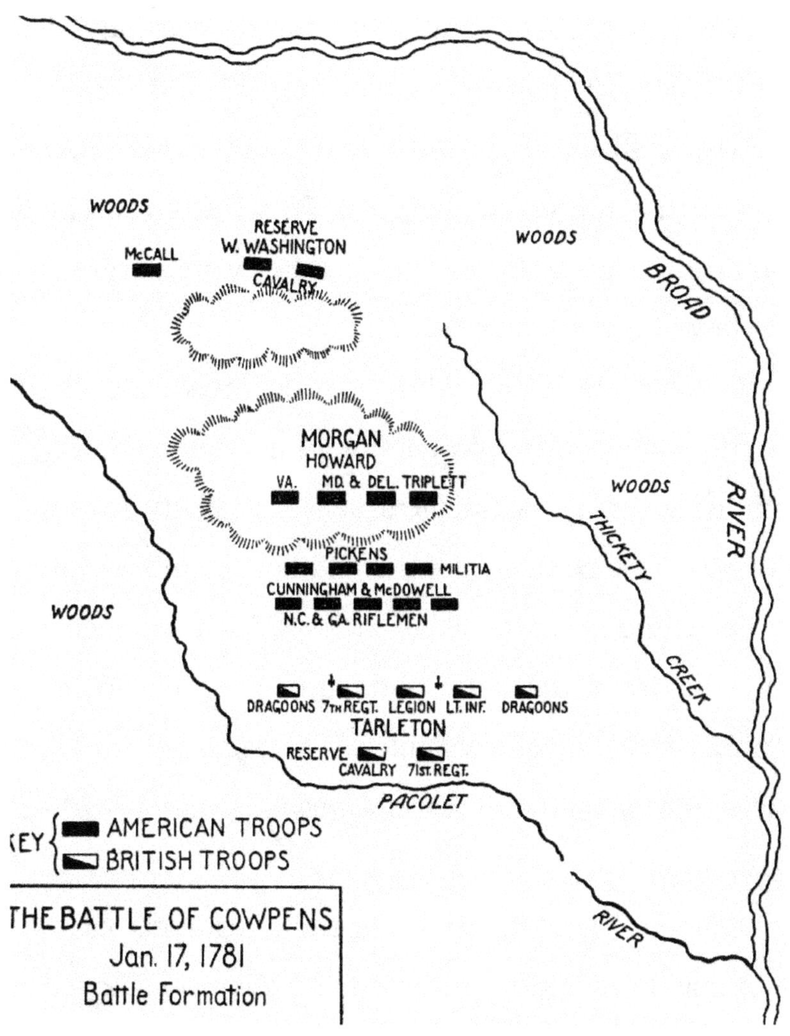

Suddenly, the sound of cannon fire erupted in front of them. *Damn, they have cannons,* John thought, convinced that each shot would weaken the militia's already shaky resolve. *They'll be fleeing our way any second.*

The artillery fire lasted a few minutes, but to John's surprise, the militia did not break. They held firm. The fire was directed at the skirmishers, but they were so spread out that few of the riflemen were hit.

Colonel Tarleton, who had deployed his British infantry and cavalry into one long line, two men deep, in front of Morgan's skirmishers, sent his cavalry forward at a trot to disperse them. John could not see the action, but he heard the sharp crack of rifles, which sounded very different from muskets, and smiled as the rifle fire continued for several minutes. *The riflemen are really giving it to them,* he thought. *Maybe the militia will fight today.*

Colonel Tarleton grew impatient with his cavalry's failure and ordered a full-on attack. His troops, over one thousand strong, advanced in two ranks at a yell. The riflemen did as they were ordered, withdrawing to the flanks of the militia line.

General Morgan was with the militia, riding back and forth in front of them as the riflemen scurried back to rejoin. With his sword raised overhead Morgan yelled, "They give us the British halloo, boys. Give them the Indian halloo, by God!" and the militia erupted in cheers and yells.

John could only see part of the militia from his position on the right side of the Continental line. He heard them yell in reaction to General Morgan, just as the British line crested the ridge where the skirmishers had been. The redcoats marched on and were soon in range of the militia—who fired deadly volleys into their ranks.

John watched as the British halted and returned fire at the militia. He expected the militia to break ranks and run, but few did so—most remained in line to fire another volley into the British.

Are they actually fighting? John thought with surprise.

The militia line held for another minute, company after company blasting a second volley into the British. Then the troops broke ranks and retreated.

"There they go," sighed John's friend Thomas, standing to his left. He nodded in the direction of the fleeing militia who were retreating toward the left flank of the Continental line. "I knew they wouldn't hold."

John was as disappointed as the others, but then he noticed that the militia wasn't fleeing in disarray but rather, in some order.

"Wait, look at them," John cried. "I don't think they're finished yet!"

Just then someone yelled, "Here they come!" and John saw the line of British redcoats appear before him, only a hundred yards away. He swallowed hard and squeezed his musket, which had been resting on his shoulder.

"Stand firm, boys," commanded Captain Wallace. "Stand firm."

General Morgan and several other mounted officers rode to the Continentals in the third line. He barked some instructions to Colonel Howard, then galloped to the left end of the line where most of the militia had fled, yelling, "Form, form, my brave fellows! Give them one more fire and the day is ours. Ole Morgan has never been beaten!"

Morgan's efforts worked, and many of the militia reformed on the left of the Continental line.

The militia had done their job well. Most had fired two aimed volleys at close range, and Tarleton's force had recoiled at their fire. Scores of British troops had fallen at the hands of the militia, and the British ranks had become disordered—but only for a moment. They were quick to dress their ranks, push forward, and force the militia back.

The British continued toward the Continental line. Some of the militia riflemen who had joined the flanks of the Continental line started firing, but the Continentals held their fire, waiting for the enemy to get closer.

General Morgan returned to the center of the Continental line, riding back and forth behind them, encouraging them to be brave and stand firm. The general's efforts gave John and his comrades confidence. One soldier would remember after the battle that Morgan's, "powerful and trumpet like voice…drove fear from every heart and gave new energy to every arm."

John stared at the approaching enemy. This was always the hardest part—the waiting, the calculating.

"Hold… Hold," ordered Captain Wallace, urging his men to hold their fire until the enemy was closer. John thought back to his first battle at Waxhaws, when his commander had waited too long to fire. *Come on, give the order,* he thought impatiently, staring at the wall of redcoats that grew larger with every step.

"Charge bayonets!" commanded a British officer as they continued toward the Continentals. All the redcoats swung their muskets down from their shoulder, holding them at their waists, bayonets pointed straight at the Continentals.

"Huzzah! Huzzah!" they yelled, in part to intimidate the Americans and in part to release the tension that they felt as they marched on.

"Make ready!" commanded Captain Wallace, ordering the men to raise their muskets and cock their flints. "Take aim!" John and his company leveled their muskets at the redcoats, who were now just fifty yards away. "Fire!"

A deafening roar erupted as John and his comrades fired their first volley. The enemy became obscured by dense smoke, but John could hear their cries of agony as the American volley hit its mark.

"Load, load!" commanded Captain Wallace, as volleys were fired further down the American line.

John reached into his cartridge box and grabbed another cartridge, his eyes peering through the thinning smoke. *Did we stop them?* he wondered as he bit into the cartridge paper to tear it open.

Suddenly, a roar of gunfire erupted in front of him as the British fired their own volley into the Americans. A musket ball whizzed past John's head, and there was a sickening thud as another struck Thomas in the chest. His lifeless body crumpled to the ground without a word.

John was horrified, but kept going. He primed his pan, poured the rest of the cartridge into his muzzle, and rammed it down the barrel, all the time staring ahead.

"Make ready," commanded Captain Wallace. "Take aim! Fire!"

John and his company squeezed their triggers and sent another deadly volley toward the enemy.

Both sides held their position, blasting volley after volley at the other for over a minute. An American cavalryman who had witnessed the fight would later recall, "When the Continentals fired, it seemed like one sheet of flame from right to left. Oh! It was beautiful."

John was aware of the screams and cries around him, but the drive to stay alive kept him focused on the task at hand—fire and reload, fire and reload.

Colonel Tarleton was surprised by the American resolve and ordered his reserve troops into battle. The 71st Battalion and part of Tarleton's cavalry were ordered to advance upon the American right flank. The British dragoons pulled ahead and moved toward the open woods to the right of the Virginians, driving away the militia riflemen who had been using the scattered trees for cover. Their departure left the American right flank exposed, and the enemy horsemen pushed forward to gain the rear of the Virginians.

They were stopped by Colonel William Washington and his cavalry, who had arrived just in time to intercept them. The two cavalry forces clashed with sabers for less than a minute before the British horsemen disengaged and withdrew.

The 71st Battalion—who had followed the British cavalry—did not retreat, however. With fixed bayonets, they advanced toward Captain Wallace's exposed right flank. Colonel Howard recognized the danger and ordered Wallace to refuse, or bend, his company to face the new threat.

"Virginians!" Wallace yelled to get his men's attention. "Right about, face!" John and his comrades did as they'd been ordered; they spun around in place and faced the rear. Wallace continued, "To the right wheel… March!"

Wallace wanted his company to turn as a line to the right, to better position themselves to protect the American right flank. When he gave the order, however, a deafening volley from the company of Maryland Continentals next to them was fired, so John and most of his company only heard Wallace shout, “March!”

The company marched straight ahead, without wheeling right as Wallace had intended.

This movement was immediately noticed by the other American companies, who figured they had missed an order to withdraw, so they faced about and marched to the rear as well.

General Morgan was furious. He confronted Colonel Howard. “What the devil is the meaning of this, Colonel?” General Morgan seethed, his face red with rage. “Who gave the order to retreat?”

Howard didn’t know, but calmed the general by pointing out that the withdrawal was orderly and to their advantage.

John and his comrades marched to the rear, many re-loading on the way. Colonel Tarleton and his men believed the Americans were quitting the field, and in their excitement, the British troops rushed after them. As they did, their own battle line became disordered.

Suddenly, Colonel Howard ordered the Continental battalion to halt and about face. He then ordered a battalion volley straight into the oncoming enemy. Nearly five hundred Continental and militia muskets were suddenly leveled at point blank range at the oncoming British.

"Fire!" commanded Colonel Howard.

The effect of the massive volley devastated the British. Scores of redcoats fell to the ground, some killed instantly, many more grievously wounded. Those not hit halted their advance, shocked by the sudden carnage.

"Charge bayonets!" ordered Colonel Howard. "Forward, march!"

John and the others yelled like madmen as they advanced forward, bayonets at the ready. Their huzzah turned into one long "Ahhhhhhh" at the top of their lungs as they closed upon the stunned enemy.

Many of the British turned and ran. Others threw down their weapons and pleaded for mercy. John encountered one such terrified soldier who had been shot in the shoulder.

“Mercy, mercy,” he begged from his knees, holding a hand over his wound to slow the bleeding.

John felt no mercy, only a desire for revenge. “Where was your mercy at Waxhaws?” he replied pointing his bayonet at the man’s chest.

“I wasn’t there, I wasn’t there!” cried the soldier.

John didn’t care. He thought of his comrades at Waxhaws and Camden and a desire to avenge them welled in his chest. He pulled his musket backwards, readying to plunge his bayonet into the soldier’s chest. The soldier flinched, bowed his head, and clamped his eyes shut, resigned to his fate. That resignation made John pause. He stared at the petrified, bloodied, soldier before him and realized he couldn’t do it. He grunted in frustration, a flurry of mixed emotions swirling inside him—shame, anger, sadness, pity—but he shoved them all aside as he lifted his musket and marched past.

Hundreds of redcoats were around John and the Continentals. Many lay on the ground, dead or wounded. Many more stood with their hands raised in surrender, muskets on the ground, dazed by what had occurred moments earlier.

We crushed them, realized John with satisfaction. He noticed a large number of enemy cavalry off in the distance, riding away from the battle. Tarleton and his horsemen had been the only ones able to escape. They rode hard to the south, pursued for a time by Colonel Washington's cavalry. There was no catching the rattled British dragoons, however, and they made their escape. Colonel Washington took possession of over thirty abandoned British baggage wagons, all loaded with much needed supplies. Tarleton's two cannons also fell into American hands.

General Morgan and his men had destroyed Banastre Tarleton's force, killing or wounding over two hundred redcoats and capturing more than five hundred. They suffered their own losses as well, however. About one hundred and fifty Americans had been either wounded or killed. Still, it was a decisive—and sorely needed—victory for the American cause.

John, however, wasn't able to see it that way. His comrades cheered around him, but John's ears were still ringing with the screams for mercy. All around him, bodies, blood. His stomach twisted at the carnage before him.

When he had fled from the Waxhaws eight months earlier and helped Colonel Porterfield off the field at Camden the previous summer, he had been largely spared the aftermath of each battle. He didn't see the shattered bodies of dead and dying men strewn about the field, many struggling in agony and begging for help. Yes, he had seen friends fall in battle, but these instances were fragmentary moments overwhelmed by his own focus of self-preservation. The worst he had witnessed up close was the wounded men at the hospital in Hillsborough. But those wounds had not been fresh.

John was overwhelmed at the scene before him at Cowpens. All his anger and hatred for the enemy disappeared in the presence of so much suffering. He caught the eye of a British soldier who'd been shot in the knee. The wounded redcoat sat upright on the ground in a daze, covering his bleeding wound with his hands.

John knelt next to him. "Here, have some water," he said, offering his canteen to the wounded man.

"Thank you," whispered the soldier. He left one hand on his knee and took the canteen with the other and drank deep from it.

"Let me cut a strip of cloth from your blanket," John said, gesturing to the cloth that was folded into a blanket roll across the soldier's chest. "We need to stop the bleeding."

The wounded soldier hesitated for a moment, unsure whether to trust John. But then he bent his head forward, allowing John to slide the blanket off. John cut a narrow strip across the top of the blanket and used it to make a torniquet for the soldier's leg. He tied it tight just above the knee and said, "Keep that tight," tapping the torniquet. "I expect a surgeon will see to you shortly."

The wounded soldier, pale and weak, only nodded in appreciation.

"Mr. Southall," yelled Sergeant Collins. "Form up with the rest of the company."

John rose and nodded toward his canteen, still in the wounded soldier's hand. "Take another drink," he said. The British soldier gratefully did so, then handed it back.

"Southall!" yelled the sergeant. John spun around quickly and headed for his company.

When he got there the soldier next to him asked, "Is that yours?" nodding toward some blood on John's sleeve.

"Not this time," John replied.

It took several more minutes for the scattered Virginians to assemble. They had lost just a few men—poor Thomas Carver, a friend of John's from Cumberland County, being one of them.

While they waited for the stragglers to join the company, John noticed groups of prisoners under guard collect the wounded of both sides. He caught sight of the soldier he had helped, his arms draped over the shoulders of two prisoners for support. They made their way toward the American camp, the soldier's wounded leg dangling as they moved.

Poor fellow, he'll lose the leg for certain, thought John.

"Where's Thomas?" asked a soldier standing in the rear rank.

John looked over his shoulder, but couldn't meet the soldier's eyes. "He didn't make it," he said sadly. The soldier shook his head, his fist clenched. "He went quickly," John added in an attempt to make the news easier to stomach.

Suddenly, Captain Wallace's voice rang out. "Take care! Shoulder firelocks!" he commanded.

It was time to return to camp and continue the march north. General Cornwallis was still out there, and his force was three times the size of Morgan's.

Chapter Seven

Williamsburg

Arnold's three week rampage up and down the James River thoroughly alarmed Virginia, but little was done to stop or even challenge him. Caught by surprise, the poorly armed Virginia militia dared not confront Arnold directly. As a result, Arnold and his force marched into Portsmouth on January 19th largely unscathed. The occupied town would serve as his base of operations for the next three months.

Outside of Portsmouth, General Peter Muhlenberg, a brigadier-general with the Continental army, commanded approximately a thousand militia posted in Suffolk and Smithfield. Too weak to directly attack Arnold—whose force had grown to eighteen hundred when his missing men finally arrived—Muhlenberg had to content himself with harassing British patrols that ventured too close to Suffolk.

General Nelson commanded the militia posted on the north side of the James River. He arrived in Williamsburg on the same day that Arnold reached Portsmouth and made the abandoned Governor's Palace his headquarters. The sparsely furnished residence was in need of repair, but it provided General Nelson with adequate space to meet and dine with his officers downstairs, and rest upstairs.

As Nelson's aide-de-camp, James was a constant presence at headquarters. He slept upstairs on a cot in a large room outside General Nelson's bedchamber, and dined with the general every day.

The general invited different officers to join him for dinner each day, and the dinner conversation James heard reminded him of life at the Raleigh Tavern.

"We should cross the river, join General Muhlenberg, and bag that damned traitor once and for all," boasted one tipsy officer at dinner.

James knew that the condition of Virginia's forces—namely, the shortage of weapons, ammunition, tents and clothing—made such bold comments sound foolish, but he kept silent and let General Nelson deal with it. Nelson nodded in apparent agreement but only said, "Perhaps we shall, perhaps we shall," before changing the subject.

Colonel Southall dined at headquarters a week after General Nelson and James had arrived in Williamsburg.

He had just returned from Hampton, where Williamsburg's militia had been sent as a precaution against Arnold. As father and son sat together with General Nelson and several other officers, James could feel his father's pride.

"Your son has proved quite indispensable, Colonel," declared General Nelson over a glass of wine. "That is, once he managed to join me."

James reddened a bit, but laughed it off. He knew General Nelson wasn't truly upset over his late arrival. His father, however, seemed worried. "I was delayed in Richmond for several days to assist Governor Jefferson," he clarified for his father's benefit. "And then, on my way to find General Nelson, I came across the fight at Hood's Point, so had to return to Richmond to warn them of Arnold's approach."

Colonel Southall smiled, relieved at the news.

"I joined Major Anderson on a patrol the night before Arnold reached Richmond," James continued, "and served under him in the battle there. It wasn't much of a fight really, they outnumbered us so…"

"He found me at Holt's Forge two days later," cut in General Nelson.

"Did you get a look at Arnold?" asked his father.

"I couldn't say, sir," replied James. "I think he stayed with the main body down on the river."

"Bloody Arnold," his father grumbled. "It's a shame about Major Anderson's tavern. Especially since business had been going so well for them."

"Yes," James said softly. "But when I left, everyone was safe. And that's what matters most."

After dinner, General Nelson allowed James to return to the Raleigh with his father and visit with his family. The next morning though, James returned to headquarters to resume his duties.

Hundreds of militia had gathered in Williamsburg in the winter of 1781, and most were quartered in the large wooden barracks behind the Governor's Palace that had been built in 1776. Some of these men had grown ill, and so in late January, General Nelson turned the West and East Advance buildings in front of the Palace into a hospital.

James was surprised to encounter Rebecca's father as he entered the Palace one morning in late January. James was on his way to the parlor with an unfinished letter when Major Anderson stepped through the front door.

"Major, sir!" cried James. "I am so gl—"

Major Anderson stepped aside with a smile and there stood Rebecca, beaming from ear to ear with joy.

James stood frozen, his mouth agape. Rebecca rushed past her father and hugged James, who lowered his arms and then gingerly returned the gesture, aware that both her father and General Nelson—who had stepped into the doorway from the parlor—could see them.

"Major Anderson, please attend to me sir," instructed General Nelson, who then turned back into the parlor to give the young couple some privacy.

James shook off his shock and squeezed Rebecca tight, then released her and stepped back to survey her. She was as beautiful as ever. "What are you doing here?" he asked.

"Father has brought us back to Williamsburg. We're staying with Uncle James," she said.

James smiled. "And your mother? How is she?"

"Everyone is well," replied Rebecca.

A brief pause ensued as they stared at each other, both simply enjoying this rare, unexpected closeness. Neither was sure how much time had passed when the pause was finally broken by General Nelson.

"Lieutenant Southall, your presence please," he called out from the parlor.

"I must go," whispered James, taking Rebecca by both hands. "But I will visit with you soon."

Rebecca gave him a smile and nodded.

James spun around and headed for the parlor while Rebecca took a seat in the central passage to wait for her father. Major Anderson didn't make her wait long, and returned from the parlor looking very determined. Rebecca leaned to the side to see if James had followed behind her father, but alas, he had not. Her father walked up to her and reached out his hand. "We must be off, dear."

Saddened that she would not get to say goodbye to James, Rebecca sighed, but accepted her father's hand. Thankfully, James was able to join the Anderson's for dinner later that afternoon, having been invited by Major Anderson before he'd departed the meeting at headquarters.

"How long will you stay here?" James asked Major Anderson at dinner.

"I don't know," he replied. "With the British in Portsmouth, it's hard to say what will happen."

"You can obviously stay as long as you wish," announced the dinner's host, James Anderson, Rebecca's uncle. "I confess it is a bit crowded with two families, but I wouldn't have it any other way."

"We thank you for that, James," Mrs. Anderson said. "You and Hannah are most kind."

After dinner, James and Rebecca crossed the street to visit with his parents at the Raleigh. The tavern was crowded with militia officers—many of whom had taken rooms in the tavern. As a result, his parents had little time to visit.

"And just imagine, your mother had to manage all of this alone while I was away," Mr. Southall said, exasperated, as he greeted them in the central passage.

"We will come again at a less busy time," replied James, patting his father on the shoulder.

"Yes, yes, please do," he replied with a regretful look.

James kissed his mother goodbye on the cheek and then took Rebecca by the hand. They stepped out onto the porch and stood there for a moment, feeling as if they'd stepped back in time.

"Let's go to our brook," Rebecca proposed. "It's still light out."

James smiled in agreement and they headed for the brook.

It had been nearly a year since Rebecca had last visited the brook, but it seemed as if it were a whole lifetime ago. "Oh, if only John were here," she sighed wistfully.

"He's somewhere in the Carolinas with General Morgan, I imagine. Not much is likely happening down there. Too cold for armies to take the field."

"I hope so," Rebecca said, wishing both boys could avoid all future battles. "And what about here?" she asked. "Do you think Arnold will attack again?"

"I doubt it," James replied. "He was fortunate to catch us by surprise when he sailed up the river, but now the entire state knows that he's here, so I think he'll stay put in Portsmouth until the spring. If he's not careful we might even capture him there. That is, if the French navy arrives."

Rebecca said nothing. She was thinking back to her encounter with Arnold in Richmond.

"What was he like?" asked James, snapping Rebecca back to the present.

"Who?" she replied, though she knew that James was asking about Benedict Arnold

"That traitor, Arnold."

"Rude and arrogant," she huffed.

"Did you tell him so?"

"Not in so many words," she replied with a grin.

James gave her a knowing smile as he imagined Rebecca scolding Arnold.

They both stood silently, listening to the running water. Finally, Rebecca said, "We best get home, the sun is setting."

James walked Rebecca home, kissed her goodnight, then headed back to the Governor's Palace, where his cot awaited him.

Three days later, Doctor Pasteur asked James to attend to him in the West Advance building, where nearly two dozen ill men were being treated. When James entered, he was surprised to find Rebecca there.

"Wh-what are you doing here?" he stammered.

Rebecca gave him a quizzical look, his tone suggested disapproval. "Just trying to help," she said. "We all must do what we can."

"She's been wonderful," added Doctor Pasteur with a smile.

But James took Rebecca by the hand and led her to a corner. "Are you sure this is wise?" he whispered. "You could bring illness home with you."

Rebecca rolled her eyes. "These boys need care, James," she said firmly. "And I mean to help provide it."

James remained worried that Rebecca might fall ill by being around the sick soldiers, but he saw her cool blue eyes harden like steel and knew she was determined to remain. He sighed and kissed her on the cheek. "You're right," he said at last. "They're lucky to have you." He gave her hand a squeeze. "I must get back," he said as he walked back to the main residence to rejoin General Nelson. *This might not be so bad,* he thought as he walked. *After all, we can see more of each other*.

With Benedict Arnold inactive in Portsmouth, and Virginia's forces too weak to attack, there was little to be done in Williamsburg but wait. Something both Rebecca and James were fine with.

Chapter Eight

Race to the Dan

Within two hours of their victory at Cowpens, General Morgan had his army on the march north. Men who had been too injured to move were left behind under a flag of truce, tended to by several doctors and volunteers who had agreed to remain.

John and his company joined the rest of Morgan's Continentals near the head of the column. They crossed the Broad River at noon and continued north. Behind them followed over seven hundred prisoners guarded by the militia, and behind those prisoners, wagons loaded with captured British arms and supplies, in addition to their own supply wagons.

The men marched off quietly—surprisingly so, given what they had just accomplished. One or two soldiers commented on the whipping they'd given the enemy, but most, John included, marched in silence, deep in their own thoughts.

John was grateful, for the first time in his life, for the long march. It gave him time to sort through his own troubling feelings.

He had emerged from the battle unscathed, as did most of his friends, and he was thankful for that. He was grateful for their victory, and knew he should feel a sense of pride—and a part of him did, it truly did. But what alarmed John was the stronger sense of regret and guilt he felt for inflicting such suffering on fellow beings. He pitied those poor men left on the battlefield, and that made him feel like a sham, a traitor.

How could he feel both pride and shame? How could he be glad to fight with his brothers in arms, proud of their victory, *and* disgusted by the actions that had made such a victory possible?

John remained lost in his thoughts well past sundown, when they finally stopped for the night and huddled around a campfire.

"That was well done today, lads," said Sergeant Collins. "But don't get too cocky. Cornwallis is still out there, and he'll be itchin' to get his boys back."

Sergeant Collins was right. When General Cornwallis learned of Tarleton's defeat at Cowpens, he immediately marched in pursuit of General Morgan. "I will have my men back," the British commander declared, "and will destroy that damn Virginian in the process!"

General Morgan and his force were in no condition to engage General Cornwallis in battle. Hampered by hundreds of prisoners and weakened by the departure of most of the Georgia and South Carolina militia—who had returned to their homes after the battle—Morgan's best strategy was to avoid Cornwallis until he was reinforced by either new militia, or the rest of the Southern army under General Greene.

When Morgan's force reached the Catawba River in North Carolina on January 23rd, he halted his Continentals, but ordered the Virginia militia—several hundred strong—to continue north with the British prisoners. Like the militia who had already departed, the Virginians were eager to return to their homes, convinced that they had done their part and that their service was up. Thus, they happily agreed to escort the prisoners to Virginia.

All that remained behind of General Morgan's detachment were his Continentals, roughly three hundred strong. And despite the grave threat Cornwallis posed, Morgan waited on the east bank of the Catawba River for instructions from General Greene, and for new militia to arrive to reinforce him.

The departure of most of the militia concerned John, and did little to help ease the confusing battle of emotions within him. But the departure of the Virginia militia presented John with an opportunity—they could deliver a letter for him. *Perhaps writing it all out will help,* he thought, *perhaps Abigail can make sense of these damned thoughts.*

So, John wrote and wrote and wrote. But no matter how he tried, he could not give voice to those conflicting thoughts. It all sounded wrong, not at all a reflection of what he *really* felt. He'd crumpled piece after piece of paper before finally giving up completely. He'd just have to push those negative thoughts deep down, focus only on the positive. The other soldiers needed him, needed him to be at his best. He couldn't let them down, not when they were risking their lives. *But the British soldiers are also risking—no,* he stopped himself. *The British soldiers are not my concern.* He took a deep breath and took out one last piece of paper. This time, he kept it short, only writing to Abigail to let her know he was alright. When he finished, he asked an officer to take it north with him.

“We’re not going to Hillsborough, but we’ll be passing nearby, so I’ll deliver it to someone in Guilford Courthouse and perhaps they’ll see that it gets to Hillsborough,” said the helpful militia officer.

After the militia departed with the prisoners, John sat down to write similar letters to Rebecca and James. He had no idea what had happened in Virginia since November, but assumed things were largely unchanged. They, of course, were not.

John and the rest of the army sat for over a week along the Catawba River in late January, then halted for nearly another week further north along the Yadkin River in early February. These long pauses puzzled John and his comrades because they believed that General Cornwallis was pursuing them. The British commander was indeed doing so, but muddy roads and flooded rivers brought his pursuit to a crawl.

General Nathanael Greene had joined Morgan on the Catawba River in late January before they retreated to Salisbury, but the rest of the American army did not come with him. Greene sent them north toward Guilford Courthouse, where he expected Morgan’s troops to eventually end up.

Hundreds of militia from North Carolina did join Morgan, but they were not enough to challenge Cornwallis, so when the flooded Yadkin River began to subside, Greene and Morgan withdrew northeast toward Guilford Courthouse. They reunited with the rest of the American Southern army there on February 9th.

It was a bedraggled collection of tired men, less than two thousand strong, that camped at Guilford Courthouse on February 10th. They were still far too weak to challenge the British, and they were made weaker by the departure of General Morgan—whose worsening illness had forced him to return to Virginia to recover.

General Greene decided that he had no choice but to continue the retreat to Virginia to seek reinforcements. The problem was that General Cornwallis was just a day's march away *and* positioned to intercept the Americans before they could reach the upper fords of the Dan River, the next big river to be crossed.

Greene's solution was to fool Cornwallis. He formed a new light corps under Colonel Otho Williams of Maryland, and ordered this detachment of seven hundred men to march north toward the fords, drawing Cornwallis in that direction.

North Carolina

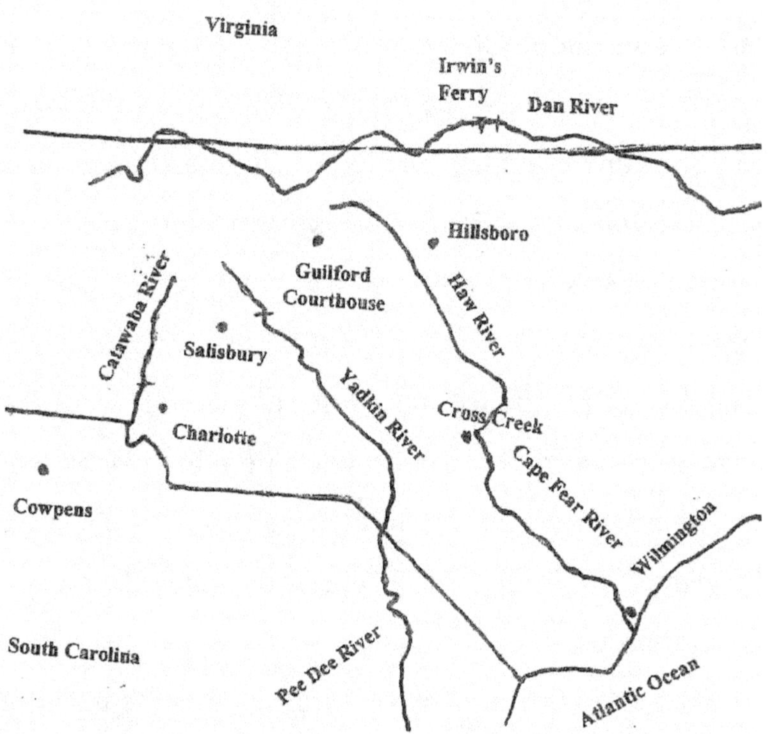

While the enemy followed the light corps, Greene planned to lead the rest of the army northeastwards toward ferry crossings—many miles downriver from the upper fords. Greene hoped that Cornwallis would pursue the light corps long enough to give the rest of his army time to reach the ferries and cross the Dan River without being attacked.

Dividing his already weak army in the face of Cornwallis's superior force was viewed by some of Greene's officers as reckless and foolish, but Greene saw it as his only chance to avoid a general battle with Cornwallis—a battle that Greene knew his troops would lose. The light corps was thus tasked to draw the British northward, while the rest of the army made its escape to the northeast.

John and his company of Virginia Continentals under Captain Wallace was part of the light corps. They marched north from Guilford Courthouse on February 10th, unaware, at first, that they would be bait for the British.

"We must be screening the rest of the army," speculated one soldier behind John. "They're probably on another road to the right of us."

John didn't give the matter much thought. They had lost General Morgan to illness, but they'd gained Colonel

Henry Lee and his noted legion of cavalry and infantry. The light corps was also double its previous size—some seven hundred strong—of infantry and cavalry, which gave John and the others a false sense of confidence.

The first day's march was long, tedious, and mostly uneventful. John thought it was odd when they didn't halt at sunset, and he grew more concerned as they marched on for several more hours. When they finally stopped, it was after nine o'clock.

"What's this about?" griped one of John's tentmates. "Marching us such a distance and halting here. Where's the camp?"

"How far you figure we marched?" asked another tentmate.

"Must have been at least thirty miles," complained the first.

John looked around and realized there were no tents to sleep in. He had assumed that they would eventually link up with the baggage wagons of the army, but the few wagons around only carried food and ammunition.

"Where are we to sleep, Sergeant?" John asked Sergeant Collins.

“Sleep?” The sergeant laughed. “Who’s going to sleep? We’ve got guard duty. Everyone report to Lieutenant Deane.”

John couldn’t believe it. They had marched for over fourteen hours and now they had to do guard duty? *This is insane,* he thought, as he made his way toward Lieutenant Deane. Deane was to command a portion of the evening guard detail, some thirty-six men who were to stand watch while the rest of the light corps rested. They were posted two hundred paces back down the road in a line of sentries across the road at intervals of forty paces per sentry. Half of the guard detail stood watch while the others rested for two hours and then replaced them.

John was selected as a sentry for the first rotation, and posted several hundred paces from the road.

“You’ll be relieved in two hours,” said Sergeant Collins sternly. “The enemy is out there, so don’t fall asleep, or you may never awaken.”

John wasn’t worried about the British—he was worried about freezing to death. While they’d marched, he had managed to stay warm, but now he had to stay in one place for two hours in the freezing cold, all without a fire to warm himself. He was exhausted and sore, and after just a few minutes of standing, his toes began to ache with cold.

"Move, move," he muttered to himself as he stamped his feet in a futile attempt to warm them and reduce the pain.

An hour into his watch, the pain had become unbearable, so John sat against a tree and removed his battered shoes and thin stockings. Blowing into his cupped hands, he squeezed his toes and rubbed his feet vigorously. It worked! The pain eventually subsided a bit and gave him a glimmer of hope that he could survive the night.

The second hour passed slowly and John was finally relieved from his post. He joined the other sentries around a campfire to warm himself properly.

"Get some sleep," scolded Sergeant Collins after a few minutes around the fire. "You'll be going back out soon enough."

John managed to doze off, his utter exhaustion overcoming the numbing cold. He was shaken awake by Sergeant Collins who announced, "Get up, boys, we march in five minutes!"

John was confused. It was still dark, and dawn seemed hours away. *Why are we marching so soon?* he wondered as he struggled to his feet.

"Let's go, grab your packs and put out the fire," ordered Sergeant Collins.

John functioned in a daze. His toes were frozen again and his feet ached, but he fell into line and started to march. His body slowly warmed from the exertion, but he was quick to take advantage of their first halt to warm his toes the way he had during his guard duty.

When the sun finally made its appearance, the mood of the men improved, and two hours after dawn they halted and were ordered to cook breakfast.

"Gladly!" muttered John as he broke from the ranks and searched for dry branches to start a fire.

Breakfast was the usual faire of salt pork and fire cakes made of cornmeal and water. As they ate their bland meal and warmed themselves by the fire, John noticed a troop of Colonel Lee's cavalry—about twenty-five horses—ride past, toward the rear of the column, and disappear down the road.

That's odd, he thought. *Where are they off to?* Within half an hour John received an answer. The distant sound of gunfire and a bugle signaled that Lee had found the enemy, or more accurately, *they* had found him.

"On your feet, boys," shouted Sergeant Collins. "Form the company."

John was surprised when the column faced away from the gunfire and started marching.

We're not going to help? he wondered, feeling bad for Lee's men.

Most of Lee's dragoons rejoined the column about an hour into the march. With them was a squad of captured enemy cavalry.

Well, it's nothing to worry about, John convinced himself. *Colonel Lee has everything under control.*

At noon, the column suddenly swung right, toward the northeast, and after another hour they halted briefly. Captain Wallace addressed the company.

"I'm sure you're wondering where the rest of the army is, especially now that we've made contact with the enemy. Well, they've been heading that way," said the captain, pointing in the direction they were now marching, "since yesterday. We've been placed between them and the enemy to protect them. It's a race, lads. We're racing the British to the Dan River. And our job is to protect the rest of the army."

John understood their task, but wasn't happy about it. Not happy at all. "Seems like we've been set up to be sacrificed, Sergeant," he complained to Sergeant Collins as they prepared to resume the march.

"Indeed, it does, lad. Indeed, it does." replied Collins, who did not seem as disappointed as John, much to John's dismay.

The light corps marched on into the night, halting only when it was reported that the British had halted.

"How close are they?" John asked one of Lee's cavalrymen as he slowly rode past.

"Too close," came the reply.

John and his comrades were spared another guard detail, and despite his growing concern for their situation, he managed to fall asleep for a few hours under a tree.

All too soon, however, he was awakened by the command to prepare to march. They pushed on all day and into the night. About two hours after sunset, they saw the glow of campfires ahead of them. John and his comrades grew sullen. They had caught up to the main army, which meant they would have to stop and fight the British while the rest of the army fled.

The light corps marched on, resigned to their fate, but when they reached the campfires, they discovered that no one was there. General Greene had departed hours earlier and had left the fires burning.

John wanted to halt and warm himself, but the enemy was too close, so the light corps kept marching. They finally halted at midnight when Lee's dragoons in the rear reported that the British had halted.

They were on the march again before dawn, and by mid-morning word had spread that General Greene and the main body of troops had reached the Dan River and was crossing.

"Just a few hours more, boys!" declared Sergeant Collins with a revigorated step. "We're almost there!"

They reached the Dan River before sunset on February 14th, and crossed over by ferryboat. Colonel Lee and a few of his dragoons were the last to cross.

"Form up, boys," ordered Sergeant Collins once the last ferryboat had been hauled ashore. "We need to find a place to stay."

The Virginians bedded down for the night in a tobacco barn about a mile from the river. Although there was no fire to warm them, John lay comfortably upon the bundles of tobacco on the floor and stared up at the empty rafters. For the first time in a week, he slept soundly.

Chapter Nine

Guilford Courthouse

James and Rebecca had no idea that John and the American Southern army had returned to Virginia. They didn't hear of it until weeks later, after General Greene recrossed the Dan River to return to North Carolina.

The situation in Williamsburg and Portsmouth had calmed considerably by February. General Arnold and his small force remained largely inactive in Portsmouth, closely watched by a thousand Virginia militia under General Peter Muhlenberg from Suffolk.

Several hundred militia were also posted in Williamsburg under General Nelson, but there appeared little need for them. This was fortunate because many were unarmed and poorly clothed. The cold winter had taken a toll on the health of many of the militiamen, and the makeshift hospital in the West and East Advance buildings next to headquarters was soon overflowing with patients suffering from influenza, pneumonia, and putrid fever (typhus).

Rebecca reported to Doctor Pasteur every morning to help as much as she could. She checked on each patient, treating their fevers with drinks of water and cool compresses on their foreheads as she listened to their stories of home. Sometimes she even wrote letters to their families for them. The shortage of medicine, however, provided a challenge, and often all Rebecca could offer them was words of encouragement as the soldiers did their best to endure their illness.

Every time she reported to the hospital, Rebecca thought of John and hoped that if he was sick or wounded, he had someone to comfort him.

James and Rebecca managed to visit each time she volunteered—which was nearly every day. Their encounters were almost always in public, so their behavior was formal and proper, but both were comforted by the daily reminder that the other was safe.

In late February, General Nelson became gravely ill and was forced to withdraw his involvement with the army. His wife came and joined him in the Palace to nurse him directly. Confined to his bedchamber upstairs in the Palace, he suffered through weeks of illness.

While General Nelson struggled to recover, James remained at headquarters, assisting Colonel James Innes, who had assumed command in Williamsburg. Innes had been the head usher at the college during James's attendance there and James respected him greatly. "He always treated me kindly," he told Rebecca one evening, "and is a good officer."

February passed slowly and in early March, James complained to Rebecca that his duties at headquarters had grown dull and monotonous.

"It could be worse," she replied. "You could be sent across the river to deal with Arnold."

"Something is brewing on that score," responded James before realizing he shouldn't have said anything.

"What? What's happening?" demanded Rebecca.

James hesitated to answer, but Rebecca's expression forced it out of him. "If the French navy shows up as is expected, we might strike at Arnold and bag him in Portsmouth. Their ships will cut off his escape by sea and then our troops can overwhelm him."

Rebecca was skeptical that Virginia's militia could overwhelm anyone—at least the troops she saw daily in Williamsburg. She didn't say that though. She just nodded.

James's complaint about his boredom of headquarters would prove premature. For the day after he voiced his complaint, General Baron von Steuben arrived in Williamsburg. And General George Weedon of Fredericksburg arrived the day after that.

James was familiar with both men. Steuben commanded all the Continental troops in Virginia, and as such, had frequent correspondence with General Nelson—much of which was written by James on Nelson's behalf. Steuben, who was a former officer in the Prussian army, had joined the American cause in 1778 and had done a great service at Valley Forge, training the American army. But his English had improved little in the ensuing years, and James found it difficult to understand him when in his company.

General Weedon had risen in the ranks of Virginia's forces from the start of the war, from lieutenant-colonel to brigadier-general. He had served admirably in New York, and at Trenton, Princeton, Brandywine, and Germantown in 1776-77, but a dispute over his rank had caused him to resign from the army in protest in 1778. He now served as a general in the militia, and his arrival, along with

Steuben's, suggested that something big was being planned.

Their arrival in Williamsburg was nothing, however, compared to the excitement produced by the arrival of General Marquis de LaFayette in mid-March.

This dashing young Frenchman, who was just twenty-three years old, created a sensation in the city when he arrived ahead of his troops, who had halted in Annapolis, Maryland. LaFayette's service to the American cause, which had begun in 1777, was well known, and it was hoped that his presence—along with the one thousand Continental light infantry he commanded, the best soldiers General Washington could spare—would bolster Virginia's militia, and help defeat Benedict Arnold in Portsmouth.

James was impressed by General LaFayette. Born of French nobility, LaFayette was complimentary and considerate to the American officers, who all respected him despite his youth.

"He makes quite an impression," James admitted to Rebecca one evening. "It's hard to believe he's just five years older than me."

Everything depended on the arrival of a French fleet, which would cut off Arnold's access to the sea. But while the Virginians waited for the French to arrive, a crucial battle erupted several hundred miles to the southwest in North Carolina.

General Greene had been in Virginia for less than a week after escaping across the Dan River in mid-February—before the promise of reinforcements had prompted him to re-cross the river and chase after his pursuer. John and his company of Virginians were still attached to the light corps, so they had crossed ahead of the main army.

Expecting the militia from Virginia to arrive any day to double his troop strength, Greene maneuvered his army to stay within striking distance of General Cornwallis.

Alas, it would take nearly a month for the expected reinforcements—two brigades of militia and one battalion of Virginia Continentals—to finally join Greene's army. When they did so in mid-March, increasing General Greene's troop strength by nearly two thousand men, he was more than ready to fight.

General Greene re-organized his army, dissolving the light corps and creating two detachments to take its place, one commanded by Colonel William Washington, and the other by Colonel Henry Lee. Captain Wallace's company was attached to Lee's detachment, which included his legion of cavalry and infantry, as well as a company of riflemen.

On the evening of March 14th, Lee's force was ordered to patrol a few miles ahead of the army, posted at Guilford Courthouse. Sometime after midnight, Lee's cavalry discovered British cavalry under Colonel Banastre Tarleton. General Cornwallis was on the march to attack the Americans, and Tarleton once again led the way.

The small skirmish that erupted between the horsemen escalated into a full-blown night battle when Lee's infantry dashed forward to join the fight, and the added firepower prompted Tarleton to withdraw. But Lee concluded that the entire British army was now coming to support Tarleton, so he wisely retreated and reported to General Greene, three miles away.

Greene was resolved to stand and fight at Guilford Courthouse, and to do so, he borrowed General Morgan's defensive tactic from Cowpens. Greene posted over a thousand North Carolina militia in his first line, supported

Battle of Guilford Courthouse

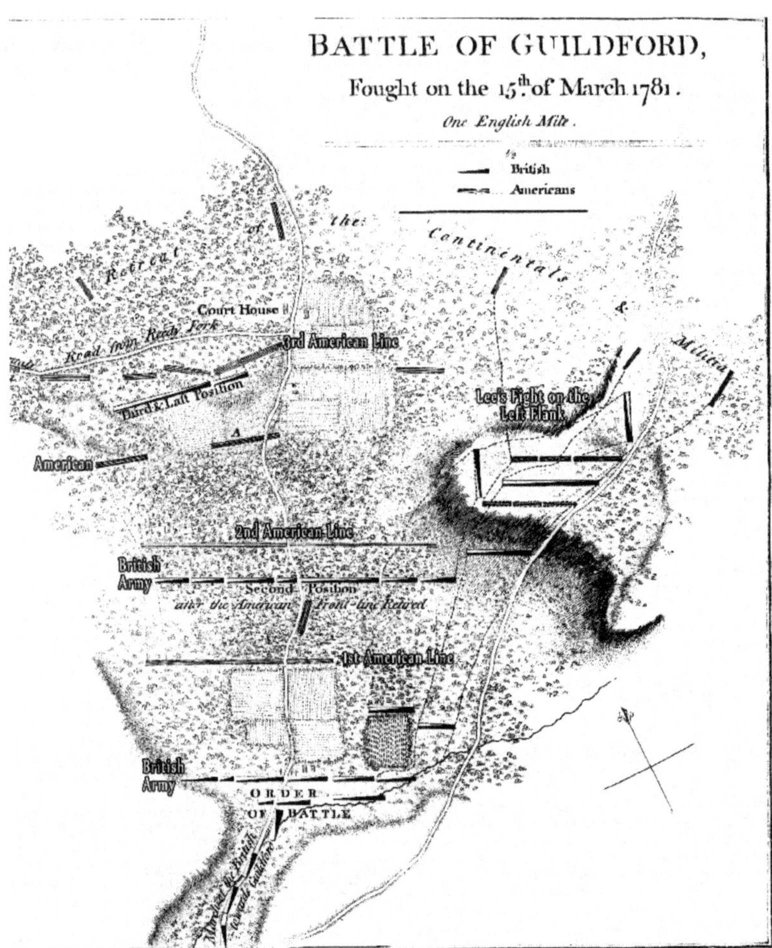

on their flanks by Colonel Washington's detachment on the right and Colonel Lee's detachment on the left.

Three hundred yards behind this first line, a second militia line of approximately twelve hundred Virginia militia were deployed in the woods, and eight hundred yards behind them, General Greene's third and final line of nearly two thousand Maryland and Virginia Continentals stood ready to replicate the success at Cowpens.

John and his company were posted with Lee's Legion infantry next to the left end of the North Carolina militia. To John's left was a company of riflemen under Colonel William Campbell, and then Lee's dragoons, which numbered around one hundred.

John felt confident about himself and the rest of the men in Lee's detachment, but he worried about the North Carolinians to his right. *Will they really fight?* he wondered. *Or will they run as the militia did at Camden?*

While John pondered what was to come, someone shouted, "There they are!" John snapped his neck toward the shout and could see the British army half a mile away, deploying for battle.

"Here we go," he muttered under his breath.

Flashes of light from several British cannons blinked at the Americans, followed a second later by the boom of cannon fire. The two American cannons posted in the road far to John's right, which bisected the American line, replied in kind, and for nearly thirty minutes, both sides fired cannon balls at each other with little effect.

The bombardment ended at 1 p.m. and the British army stepped off, nearly two thousand strong, directly toward the Americans. John watched in awe as a wall of British redcoats and Hessians—German troops allied with the British—marched in unison across the plowed fields. *They certainly know what they're doing,* he conceded.

"Hold your fire, boys! Let them get closer!" came the command from the officers in the rear. The tension was almost unbearable, but John understood why they had to wait. Musket fire from over a hundred yards away rarely hit its target and was thus nothing but a waste of ammunition. John knew this—but it didn't ease the tension he felt as he waited for the British to come within range.

A handful of scattered musket shots rang out from those who couldn't stand the wait, but everyone in John's company held their fire at the urging of the officers.

When the British were about one hundred fifty yards away, however, whole companies of militia began firing. This triggered a massive volley from the rest of the militia line—which luckily staggered the British. Their advance stopped, but only for a moment. After a brief pause, the British continued forward, led by a brave officer urging them on.

John and the men around him had held their fire, waiting for their officers to give the command. The command finally came once the enemy was within a hundred yards. "Make ready, take aim, fire!" John methodically aimed, pulled the trigger, and hurried to re-load.

Out of the corner of his right eye he noticed movement. The militia were fleeing after just one shot. Not all of them, but most of them.

"Damn!" he swore. *They're running away again.*

"Make ready! Take aim! Fire!" came the hurried command again, just fifteen seconds after the first. John and his comrades held firm and fired another shot into the oncoming wall of enemy soldiers.

The collapse of the militia in the center of the first American line forced the units of the flanks to withdraw as well. Colonel Lee's detachment, joined by about one hundred militia, withdrew orderly, unlike the rest of the North Carolina militia. But Lee and his men were being pursued by a battalion of British Guards who had yet to fire their muskets. The redcoats pressed forward relentlessly, bayonets leveled.

Lee's men withdrew into nearby woods at an angle that separated them from the rest of the American army. The wooded terrain also prevented them from maintaining a solid line, so when they halted to face the enemy, they broke into small groups and used the trees to cover themselves against the British.

John heard Captain Wallace give the order for independent fire, allowing each soldier to fire as fast and as often as he pleased. John leveled his musket at a small group of approaching redcoats and fired, then ducked behind a tree and furiously reloaded.

All around him his comrades did the same, and a steady roar of musketry filled the air. Suddenly, a piece of bark whizzed past John, and he realized the British were firing back. He swung around to face them and looked for a target. He'd never fought this way before, deliberately searching for someone to shoot. Every shot he'd fired previously had been part of a volley with sixty other men, where they all just leveled their muskets and fired downrange at the approaching enemy. Somehow, firing in volleys didn't feel personal, but as John scanned the terrain in front of him to find someone to shoot, he suddenly felt guilty for doing so.

His vision blurred as he tried to focus on the bodies before him. *It's me or them,* he thought, shaking his head to clear his vision, and hopefully, his conscience.

Finally, John's eyes focused on a redcoat about forty yards away. He was slightly to the right and reloading his musket next to a tree, seemingly unaware of the danger he was in. John took careful aim, breathed deep, and fired. Immediately after, he darted back behind the tree to reload. He didn't check to see if he'd been successful—part of him didn't want to know.

I hope I only wounded him, he thought as he rammed down his next load and returned his rammer. He swung back around the tree to find another target.

All around him, his comrades did the same, and the British troops, who were not accustomed to such fighting, began to waver. John was not aware, but some of the

Virginia militia on the second line had also joined the fight, hitting the British on their flank.

But just as the British troops broke and withdrew, a regiment of Hessians arrived to help them. They took the place of the redcoats, whose officers tried to reform them behind the Hessians, but it was no use. The Hessians began dropping just as fast as the British had.

The confused and bloody fight continued for several more minutes, ending only when Colonel Lee disengaged and ordered his troops to withdraw toward the third American line.

John headed for the rear and came across three men huddled around an officer lying against a tree.

My God, it's Captain Wallace, John realized with a start.

"He's dead," announced one of the men crouching next to the captain. "There's nothing to be done for him."

John felt his stomach tighten, his breath catch in his throat.

"Let's go!" ordered Sergeant Collins. "We've been ordered to withdraw!"

John was numb, his legs felt rooted to the ground, but somehow he was moving, following his comrades to the rear.

Most of the riflemen with Lee, however, lingered—perhaps due to overconfidence, or perhaps because they just didn't hear the order. Whatever the reason, they paid a heavy price for staying, because as Lee left, Colonel Banastre Tarleton arrived with his dragoons and charged at the remaining riflemen. Many were cut down, and those who had miraculously managed to escape blamed Colonel Lee for deserting them. Lee would counter that he had simply been following his orders to reform on the third line once the enemy broke the first American line.

By the time Lee and his men reached the American third line, the bulk of the fighting had ended. It had been a vicious fight, the outcome of which hung in the balance for several excruciating minutes. After they had fought their way through two American lines, the weakened British army now had to confront a fresh third American line of Continentals—typically the best soldiers America had.

The first British attack on this line ended in disaster, but a second advance scattered a Maryland regiment, and the fight then became hand to hand.

When the Maryland troops fled, General Greene ordered a withdrawal, insisting that preserving the army took priority over winning a single battle.

John and his comrades arrived just as the American retreat began, and they were ordered to form a rear guard. This, however, would prove to be unnecessary because Cornwallis's army, although victorious in battle, was shattered and in no condition to pursue the Americans. Cornwallis had started the day with nearly two thousand men. By the end of the battle, over a quarter of them had fallen or been killed or wounded in the fierce fight. Cornwallis's losses included many of his best officers.

General Greene's army also suffered casualties, with some two-hundred-sixty men killed and wounded, and over a thousand, mostly militia, missing. But Greene had started with over four thousand four hundred men, and the core of his force, the Continentals, were still sound. They retreated ten miles to Speedwell's Furnace, an ironworks on Troublesome Creek. They would remain there for several days, waiting for Cornwallis to act.

The day after the battle, Abigail and her father arrived in camp to help tend to the wounded. They had learned of the battle early that morning, and rushed to the ironworks to help as best they could. John learned of their arrival by chance, while visiting a friend who had been shot in the arm.

"Abigail?" he said with a start when he passed her in the makeshift hospital. "What are you doing here?"

Abigail was just as surprised to see John. But her surprise turned to concern as she eyed him. "John, are you alright?" she asked.

"Yes, yes, I'm fine. Not a scratch on me." He spun around to prove it. "I was just visiting a friend," he clarified. "What are *you* doing here?"

"Father and I have come to help," she replied. "We learned of the fight this morning and hurried here."

"We could certainly use the help. It was an awful fight," John admitted. "Captain Wallace was killed."

"Poor man," Abigail frowned, her hand on her heart. "But you're sure you're alright?" she asked again.

"I'm fine," John insisted, "though I'm beginning to think Tarleton has it out for me, for I've learned he was who we fought against yesterday."

Abigail grinned. "You do seem to always be up against him, don't you?"

Just then Doctor Jenkins called for Abigail. “I have to go,” she said hurriedly. “Come see me later tonight. I’ll be here.”

John nodded and watched her leave. He turned with a smile and proceeded out of the hospital.

“What are you so happy about?” asked Sergeant Collins when John returned to his company.

“Oh, nothing,” he replied. “Just glad for another day.”

Sergeant Collins shook his head—not believing a word of it.

At the end of the day, John asked the sergeant if he could return to the hospital.

“Are you sick?” Sergeant Collins asked.

“No, just want to visit someone.”

“A patient, or someone else?” Collins asked suspiciously.

“Miss Jenkins and her father,” John admitted sheepishly. “They arrived this afternoon to help.”

“So, *that’s* what the smile was about,” Sergeant Collins chuckled. “Yes, you can go. But you best be back before retreat is sounded.”

John found Abigail and Doctor Jenkins eating with another doctor in a corner of the hospital.

"Good evening, sir," John said with a small bow.

"Good evening, Mr. Southall. I'm very glad to see that you escaped from the fight unharmed."

"And I am pleased to see you again, sir. I'm sure your help is greatly appreciated."

"You may be seeing much more of me, son," responded Doctor Jenkins. "I've decided to remain with the army for the time being. Of course, Abigail will remain as well," he added with a knowing smile.

"The army is fortunate to have you both," replied John with a smile of his own.

"I wish we could continue our visit," Doctor Jenkins said as he rose, "but we have work to do. Please excuse us."

Abigail gave her father a resigned pout, and a frown that John assumed translated to "I'm sorry," but followed her father back to the patients in the hospital. John bowed as they passed and returned to his camp, disappointed.

With nearly two hundred wounded men to care for, Abigail had little time to visit with John. Still, he was thrilled that she was in camp. *We'll be together soon enough,* he told himself.

That evening John dreamed not of Abigail, as he had hoped, but the British soldier he had shot at. "Why?" the soldier kept saying, his bloody hands covering a belly wound. "Why?" The blood oozed over his fingers. "Why?" he coughed, blood sputtering from his mouth, his mouth suddenly slack, eyes suddenly black and—

John woke with a start, covered in sweat, his heart racing. He wiped the sweat from his brow and took several deep breaths. *It was him or me,* he thought, closing his eyes. *Him or me, him or me, him or me,* was the refrain that played as he drifted back to sleep.

Unfortunately, but not unsurprisingly, John saw little of Abigail over the next few days. And when the orders came to break camp, he learned that she and her father were staying behind.

"We're going to stay with the wounded for a while longer," she explained. "Then we'll come and join you."

Neither of them knew it at the time, but General Greene had decided to march back to South Carolina to threaten the British there. Greene expected that General Cornwallis would follow him, but Cornwallis marched to Wilmington instead, and would remain there for a month to rest his battered army and determine how best to proceed.

While Cornwallis sat in Wilmington, and Greene marched toward South Carolina, the situation in Virginia was deteriorating for the Americans.

The plan to capture General Benedict Arnold in Virginia had suffered a blow in late March when instead of the French navy, a squadron of British warships arrived in Virginia. They were part of a large British reinforcement sent by General Clinton in New York.

The arrival of these reinforcements, some twenty-five hundred British troops under General William Phillips, as well as the additional warships that protected the transports, ended all hope of an American attack on Arnold in Portsmouth. Thus, General LaFayette reluctantly returned to Annapolis and prepared to rejoin General Washington's main army in New York. And Virginia's leaders were left to prepare themselves for the inevitable—a new British offensive in the state, this time against four thousand five hundred British troops.

Governor's Palace

Chapter Ten

The British Occupy Williamsburg

General Phillips, who had assumed command of all British forces in Virginia upon his arrival, began his operations with a naval raid up the Potomac River in early April. The reports of British privateers (American sailing vessels in service to the British) raiding both shores of the Potomac River all the way to Alexandria, alarmed Virginia's leaders for there was little they could do to stop them.

General Weedon, who had remained in Williamsburg in command of the militia while bedridden General Nelson continued to recover, had been ordered to Fredericksburg in mid-April to assume command of militia there.

Colonel Innes had assumed command of the militia around Williamsburg upon Weedon's departure, and on April 18th, received reports from Newport News that a large British fleet had been sighted making its way up the James River. The main British offensive had begun.

With General Nelson still too weak to take the field, James served as Nelson's liaison to Colonel Innes. He accompanied the colonel to Burwell's Ferry on the river, just four miles from Williamsburg. With the help of a spy glass, they could just barely make out several sailing vessels far down the river. James wasn't certain they were British, but Colonel Innes, convinced by the reports from Newport News, concluded that they were. He took a slip of paper and a pencil from a pouch and began writing.

When he finished, he turned to James. "Lieutenant, take this order back to town and deliver it to your father. We need to remove our supplies as quickly as possible. Tell him to have them transported to York. Then see to General Nelson and help him prepare to leave."

James rode hard for Williamsburg upon Spartan. He found his father at the Raleigh and delivered the message, then rushed to warn Rebecca and her family of the British approach. Mr. Anderson and his brother were not home, but the rest of the family was.

"You and your family should leave tonight," James urged.

"Nonsense!" Rebecca replied. "I'm to be at the hospital tonight and I intend to be there! I've faced down the redcoats before."

James didn't have time to argue, he had to get to the Governor's Palace and warn General Nelson. But he had to try. "Don't be foolish, Becca," he said. "It's safer for you and your family to leave."

"We're not going anywhere," said Mrs. Anderson, who had overheard the discussion in the hallway on her way down the stairs. "We're staying here to ensure no damage comes to this place."

Rebecca gave James a smug smile. But seeing the fear in his eyes, her expression softened. "Wait," she said. "I'll ride with you to the hospital."

They rode double upon Spartan to the Palace in silence. Rebecca thought about apologizing, but it never sounded right in her head. She *wasn't* sorry about staying behind to help at the hospital. But she was sorry that her actions had upset James. As for James, he knew it was pointless to argue with Rebecca when she had already made up her mind. There was simply nothing to say.

When they passed the gate, they separated without saying a word to each other, Rebecca heading to the West Advance and James into the main residence.

"General, sir," James said as he entered General Nelson's room, "we need to leave. The British are sailing up the river."

General Nelson rose from his bed and eased himself to its edge. “How close are they?” he asked.

“Colonel Innes is at Burwell’s Ferry and can see their ships,” replied James. “He’s having the supplies moved to York.”

“No,” said the General. “Not York. They need to go to New Kent.” He forced himself up from the bed, went to his desk, and began writing. It was an order countermanding Colonel Innes, instructing that all the military stores in town be taken to New Kent and West Point.

“Take this to your father,” he said, handing James the order. “We’ll take the weapons, powder, and whatever sick can travel in wagons to New Kent. Load the cloth, tents, and other gear aboard the schooner at Capital Landing and have it sail to West Point.”

“I understand, sir,” James replied with a bow. He stopped at the West Advance to tell Rebecca and attempt once more to convince her to leave with the sick, but she once again refused.

“I’m not going anywhere, James!” she shot at him, arms crossed. “Some of these men are too sick to move.”

He supposed it was admirable, her compassion. And he *did* admire it—it was one of the things he loved most about her. But in this moment, all James wanted was to ensure Rebecca's safety, and he knew she would be much safer if she evacuated. He pleaded at her with his eyes, but that determined gleam never left her own. So, James sighed in resignation, kissed Rebecca on the cheek, and left to deliver General Nelson's order to his father.

"I understand," responded his father upon receiving his instructions. "I need to send a rider to Colonel Innes immediately," he said to James, "to inform him of the change."

James shook his head. "I can't," he said. "I need to return and assist General Nelson." He paused, lowered his voice. "What of mother and the others?"

It was his father's turn to shake his head. "She refuses to go. She's going to do all she can to protect the tavern. There's no convincing her otherwise."

James sighed. "I'm not surprised. The Andersons are doing the same."

Father and son half-smiled at each other, then the colonel remembered his task and cleared his throat. "Right, off with you then, Lieutenant."

James bowed to his father, who returned the honor, and departed. He returned to the Palace and found General Nelson directing a servant to pack up his belongings.

"Lieutenant," he said when he spotted James, "go and pack your things now. We'll send them to New Kent with my things. Keep a change of clothes and other necessaries in your portmanteau, but pack the rest in my chest."

"Yes, sir."

"We are nearly done here," General Nelson reported when James returned with his things. "Go and check on how Doctor Pasteur is doing with the sick."

James was more than happy to do so—it gave him another chance to talk to Rebecca. When he entered the West Advance, he saw that some of the cots were now empty and the chest of medicinal supplies had been removed, but there were still fifteen men scattered about on cots.

"These are the men who are too ill to move," explained Doctor Pasteur. "I will stay here and tend to them."

"And I will remain to help," Rebecca added, having overheard the doctor as she re-entered the building.

James frowned at her, but then said, "Yes, yes. I know."

Rebecca thought she would feel a sense of accomplishment, having won their argument, but instead she felt hollow. She took a step closer to him, her hand outstretched, but James stepped back. She let her hand drop. "The others are all loaded into wagons and are ready to go," she said softly.

James gave only a curt nod. "Very good," he said. "We shall leave shortly." He turned and left the West Advance.

General Nelson appeared at the doorway of the Palace and James, realizing that the general was still very weak and needed help with the stairs, sprinted over to him to guide him to his coach. Mrs. Nelson was not with him; she had returned home to tend to the children.

"Thank you, Lieutenant," General Nelson said as he leaned on James and descended the stairs, apparently unaware of Doctor Pasteur and Rebecca's decision to remain behind.

"I shall ride alongside the coach, sir," said James as he handed General Nelson off to his servant at the gate. He then turned to the West Advance and looked at Rebecca, who stood resolute in the doorway, a small, unsure smile on her face.

Damn stubborn girl, thought James. But he returned her smile, then nodded goodbye and headed for the stables to fetch Spartan.

The column of wagons commenced its journey to New Kent before 7 p.m. They travelled slowly all night and reached the courthouse at 4 a.m. General Nelson had slept most of the way, but James had been unable to sleep and was exhausted.

Both men shared a room at a tavern across from the courthouse, and James thankfully managed to catch a bit of sleep there. When he awoke at sunrise, he found General Nelson sitting in a corner chair, waiting for him to stir.

"I trust you are now well enough rested to begin," Nelson said. James snapped awake and sat up, blinking the sleep out of his eyes. "I need you to return to Williamsburg and find Colonel Innes. Update him on our move and remain with him until the enemy's intentions are clear. And be sure to get something to eat before you leave."

"Yes, sir," James replied as he stood to dress. Within the hour, he was on the road to Williamsburg, and by noon, back in the former capital. He found Colonel Innes at the Courthouse, preparing to ride out to Burwell's Ferry.

"Lieutenant Southall," said the colonel. "I trust the general is well in New Kent."

"He is, sir. He sent me back to learn the latest."

"Well, we shall learn it together," replied Innes. "I'm heading for Burwell's now."

When they arrived at Burwell's Ferry, they could see plainly that several armed ships were escorting over a dozen flat bottomed boats loaded with infantry up the river.

"How long until they reach us?" asked James, trying to hide his nervousness.

"It looks like the tide is against them presently. They might not even land here. They may pass us by, like Arnold did."

"But if they do land, when do you think they'll do it?' James pressed.

Innes thought a moment. "By the time the tide turns in their favor, I don't think they'll have enough daylight to land. So, it will likely be tomorrow."

James swallowed hard. "What shall we do?"

"We'll try to stop them!" answered Colonel Innes with a laugh.

James nodded. *Of course, of course we will try to stop them,* he thought. He tore his eyes away from the ships and steeled his nerves. "What can I do to help?"

Innes paused and looked at James. "Report to your father. He's over there in the earthwork. Tell him you've been detached to his command for the time being."

"Thank you, sir," James replied with a smile.

Colonel Innes's prediction about the British would prove to be correct. The British were unable to get into position in time to land troops that day, so they anchored and waited—leaving James and about two hundred militia waiting at Burwell's Ferry through the cold night.

That night, James realized the date: April 19th. *It's been six years since this all started,* he thought in disbelief. *Six years of war*. He shivered in the cold, feeling heavy under the weight of his realization. He wasn't sure when he finally dozed off, but he awoke with a start at dawn.

The enemy was now clearly visible, their vessels scattered about in Burwell Bay, some just a few hundred yards from shore.

"What's happening, Father?" asked James, confused by the British inaction.

“I’m not sure, son. The tide is in their favor if they want to proceed up the river, but they’ve stayed put. It looks like they intend to land here. I think they are waiting for more vessels to arrive.”

Colonel Southall’s observation was correct. General Phillips had two vessels full of calvary that had yet to arrive. When they finally did so, sometime after noon, he proceeded to land his troops.

James watched with his father and Colonel Innes as part of the enemy fleet set sail up river. At the same time, dozens of longboats full of soldiers rowed toward shore. They were escorted by a single British gunboat, which methodically fired a six-pound cannon at the Virginians every thirty seconds. One of the shots passed close by, and James noted the peculiar whir as the cannon ball flew overhead and crashed into a tree. James had spent two years in the militia, but this was the first time he had come under fire. He was nervous, but ultimately more concerned about appearing unafraid than about being shot.

Suddenly, James’s father pointed toward the long boats. “They’re turning downriver!” he shouted. The gunboat, which up to that point had fired only six-pound cannonballs one at a time, switched to grapeshot. This was more terrifying because instead of one cannonball flying toward them, twenty grape-sized lead balls were fired at once. They spread out in a wide pattern, increasing the chance of striking multiple people.

A second after the gunboat fired its first round of grapeshot, the ground in front of the earthwork that was protecting James and the others seemed to explode as the grape sized lead balls plowed into it, throwing dirt into the air, but not striking anyone.

James had ducked instinctively, but then stood quickly to mimic his father, who hadn't budged at the shot.

"They're going to land below and flank us," realized Colonel Innes. The British gunboat fired another shot, but it was aimed to the left of the earthworks, and scoured the ground and brush.

"They're trying to keep us from moving to challenge their landing," declared Colonel Southall. "They want us to stay here."

Once the British troops reached shore, Colonel Innes decided it was futile to stay. "They outnumber us, and can come in from behind if we stay here," he said as he ordered the militia to withdraw to Williamsburg.

James rode ahead of the withdrawing troops, heading straight to the West Advance of the Governor's Palace to alert Rebecca about what was about to unfold. She was tending to a patient when he entered, and the look on James's face told her the British were on their way.

"I just can't," she said as he approached. "These men need me. I know you're worried, but I'll be alright, James, I promise. I stood up to them before and survived."

"I'm not going to try to convince you to leave," James told her. "I just wanted to see you again. To tell you I am proud of you, that I admire your compassion and determination. These men are fortunate to have your help." He reached for her, and Rebecca fell into his arms. When she pulled away, James's shirt felt wet.

Rebecca swiped the tears from her eyes. "Sorry," she chuckled, noticing the wet spot.

James shook his head and smoothed her hair to try and calm her. "I have to warn our families," he said. "I may not have time to return. Be careful, Becca. This is probably just another raid and they will soon be gone. But please, don't go and do anything crazy while they're here."

Rebecca laughed. "I won't," she promised.

James hugged her once more. “I love you,” he said into her neck.

“And I love you,” she whispered back, hugging him tighter.

They separated and James dashed to his horse. He found his mother and Mrs. Anderson still determined to stay as well. There was no convincing them otherwise.

As he was leaving the Anderson’s home, Colonel Innes rode up, his troops still a mile behind.

“We’re marching on, Lieutenant,” he announced. “The enemy is also landing at Jamestown, and they intend to approach from both directions and trap us here. I refuse to allow that. They can have the town, but not my troops. We’re withdrawing toward New Kent.”

“Yes, sir,” replied James.

“I want you to ride ahead to New Kent and inform General Nelson. I don’t know if the enemy will pursue, but he needs to be aware of the possibility, in case we need to retreat further.”

“I understand, sir,” James said. He kicked Spartan hard and rode off, thinking of Rebecca the whole way. Behind him marched the militia, who had passed through

Williamsburg and halted six miles outside of town, out of the grasp of the British.

Rebecca, Mrs. Southall, Mrs. Anderson, and the rest of Williamsburg's residents, had been left to face the British alone.

The British entered the city at 5 p.m., hundreds of red and green coated troops, with cavalry. The men wearing green coats were actually American loyalists fighting for the Crown; the Queen's Rangers, under Colonel John Simcoe. The troops in redcoats were British regulars, many with long experience with the army.

Most of the townsfolk shut themselves indoors, hoping to not draw the invaders' notice. General Phillips, accompanied by General Arnold, led the main body of enemy troops into Williamsburg. They rode past the abandoned capital and down Duke of Gloucester Street.

"Have your dragoons search the entire town, Colonel," Phillips instructed Simcoe as they rode past the Raleigh Tavern.

The British commanders stopped at the Courthouse and dismounted. General Phillips ordered that strong guards be posted on every road into town, and when he learned that a large barracks stood behind the Governor's

Palace, ordered that the troops be quartered there for the evening.

Doctor Pasteur and Rebecca were standing in the doorway of the West Advance when General Phillips, General Arnold, and their entourage entered the front gate.

"General, sir," Doctor Pasteur said with a nod. "We have over a dozen sick men inside and ask for your protection."

"And you are Doctor…?"

"Pasteur, sir."

Rebecca stood partially hidden behind the doctor, but caught General Arnold's eye. There was a flash of recognition that alarmed Rebecca, so she looked away immediately, not wanting to encounter him again.

General Phillips considered the situation, then said, "Well, Doctor Pasteur, you have our protection. Is there anything your patients need?"

"Thank you, sir," replied the doctor with a bow. "But we are well provisioned with medicine." This was not true, but Doctor Pasteur did not wish the general to be aware of the true state of things within the militia—namely, that there was a shortage of everything. His patients mostly needed time to recover in peace. There was little that 18th century medicine could do for them.

"Might you suggest a residence I may quarter in, doctor? This place," he said with a frown as he looked around, "looks sort of run down."

Doctor Pasteur was caught off guard by the question and did not immediately answer, but Rebecca stepped forward and volunteered the Carter residence, right next to the Palace. Dudley Digges of Yorktown had rented the building for several years, but when the government had moved to Richmond, he'd vacated, leaving the original furnishings that had belonged to its landlord, Robert Carter, behind.

General Phillips turned to an officer and directed him to investigate the Carter house. He then looked to Rebecca and thanked her with a nod. Her face reddened and she caught General Arnold staring intently at her, his eyes dark. She stepped back, once more using Doctor Pasteur as a shield.

The officers went into the Palace, aware that it had been the headquarters of the rebels. They briefly looked about, and then returned to the entrance to wait. When the officer who'd been sent to check on the Carter house returned, he reported that although the house was a bit dusty inside, it was adequately furnished and would serve nicely for the general's quarters.

"Very well then, have my baggage delivered there," ordered General Phillip. He then turned to General Arnold and said, "General, I wish for you to quarter on the other side of town. So that we may react faster if the rebels surprise us."

The officers attending the two generals smiled wryly. They knew that was not the only reason Phillips desired Arnold to quarter so far away. Another, perhaps stronger reason, was that Phillips *despised* Arnold—as did most British officers—and wished to keep him as far away as possible. General Arnold likely knew this, but nodded his acknowledgment with a stoic expression and sent an aide to procure quarters. Arnold then excused himself and walked down the steps, turning right toward the West Advance.

Doctor Pasteur was in another room, and Rebecca was tending to a patient, her back to the door, so she didn't notice Arnold at first. Not until he walked up to her and cleared his throat to get her attention.

Rebecca whirled in surprise. Arnold was staring at her, eyes narrowed in concentration. "We have met, haven't we," he said, not as a question but a confirmation. "I just can't remember where."

"You burned my father's tavern in Richmond," Rebecca replied coldly.

"Yes, yes, it *was* Richmond." Arnold said, pleased at himself for remembering. "But *I* didn't burn your tavern. Misfortune is to blame, or the winds that blew the flames toward it. I was just doing my duty."

"Your duty?" Rebecca said incredulously. "It is your duty to burn people's homes and deprive them of their livelihood?" She crossed her arms and glared. "Not a very honorable duty, sir." Arnold said nothing, so Rebecca continued. "But I guess I should expect such conduct from the likes of you."

Arnold had had enough and turned to depart. He was not about to let a woman, a *girl* really, get the better of him, he *would* control his temper. He took a deep breath and when he had steadied himself, paused at the door and looked back at Rebecca. "I do deplore your loss, miss, but it was the cost of war. Nothing else." He then disappeared out the door.

In the evening, Rebecca and Doctor Pasteur took shifts tending to the sick. They were assisted by three enslaved women, Lucy, Sarah, and Sarah's twelve-year old daughter, Dinah. The women had been seized by the government of Virginia as the property of a Tory in 1776, and assigned to several people over the years until they had at last ended up in the charge of Doctor Pasteur.

Sarah and her daughter tended the kitchen, while Lucy helped with the patients. They all stayed above the kitchen at night, and on this night, they found themselves talking about freedom.

"Maybe we should run," Lucy whispered. "Governor Dunmore freed us all before he left."

Lucy was referring to Dunmore's proclamation in November 1775, in which he'd offered freedom to any runaway slave of a rebel who would fight for him. In truth, his offer had never applied to women—nor to enslaved people held by loyalists—but over time, the proclamation had become misunderstood by many.

"What if the redcoats don't take us though?" asked Sarah. "They haven't said anything about freedom, and I haven't noticed anyone else running to them."

"Well, I'm just saying maybe we ought to try," countered Lucy, who didn't have a daughter to think of.

"You can if you want, but I got Dinah with me now, and I won't risk losing her. Not even for freedom."

Lucy frowned in reply. "Well, I can't go it alone." And with that, the idea was pushed aside for the evening, and they eventually fell asleep.

Rebecca woke at dawn and got straight back to work. Over twenty men had died of illness since she had begun caring for the sick in February—but none had died in the last two weeks, and she was determined to keep it that way. Rebecca checked on each patient and brought the doctor to the ones she was most concerned about. Making them as comfortable as possible was her chief goal. Nature and time would hopefully take care of the rest.

Several other women from the town reported to the hospital to assist over the course of the morning, and this allowed Rebecca to return home for the afternoon and dine with her family. On the way, she heard talk that the British had raided Yorktown.

According to one account, British cavalry had ridden by cover of night to Yorktown and caught the garrison by surprise. Most had fled and escaped in the dark, but many others had been caught and forced to give their parole, which was a pledge to no longer fight before they were released. The punishment for violating one's parole was severe, sometimes even death, so it was a pledge that most men kept.

Rebecca thought of James and her father. *They went to New Kent. I wonder if any redcoats went to New Kent last night, too.*

In the afternoon, a British doctor arrived at the hospital to offer his assistance. He consulted with Doctor Pasteur, who showed him several patients, then sent a soldier to his tent to retrieve some medicine.

As Rebecca passed the Courthouse, she saw people staring and pointing toward the direction of the Palace. She turned and saw great billows of smoke rising in the sky. "Oh my God," she stammered as she ran back to the green to get a better view.

When she arrived, she heard someone say, "They're burning the barracks!" and relief washed over her. She had feared the Palace itself, and thus maybe the hospital, had caught fire.

Rebecca began to worry that General Phillips meant to do what Arnold had done in Richmond. *Would he torch the*

Palace, the Magazine, the Courthouse? If Arnold is in charge, she concluded, *probably so, but perhaps General Phillips will be less destructive.* Then a different thought struck her. *Oh my, what of Uncle James's furnaces?*

She turned and ran down Duke of Gloucester Street, searching the sky as she ran. *There's no smoke, thank God.*

When Rebecca reached her uncle's house, however, she found a large party of British soldiers destroying the buildings that had formerly housed the armory—the armory that had been transferred, and burned, in Richmond.

Sure enough, General Arnold was there, overseeing the destruction. The buildings and furnaces inside them had been pounded into unusable pieces.

Arnold saw Rebecca and gave her a mocking bow. "We wanted to burn them," he said, "but were afraid the house and town would catch fire."

Rebecca glared at the traitor, flames in her eyes, but she was relieved that the house had been spared. After dinner she returned to the hospital for what she hoped would be an uneventful night.

She was awakened in the morning by the sound of the British army preparing to march. General Phillips's main objective had been to capture the militia posted at Williamsburg. Having failed that, he had decided to move on, destroying what little public property there was, like the barracks and former armory buildings—property that could be useful to the rebels.

General Phillips marched his force to the Chickahominy River where his ships had gathered. It took several hours for the men and horses to be re-boarded, after which Phillips sailed further upriver. His destination was a much larger war prize than Williamsburg, an important supply depot on the Appomattox River, the town of Petersburg.

Chapter Eleven

A Very Active Spring

On the day the British re-boarded their ships on the Chickahominy, Colonel Innes's troops and their baggage wagons crossed the Pamunkey River. Although General Nelson was not ready to return to the field with his troops, he did feel well enough to ride to Richmond to meet with Governor Jefferson and discuss strategy in response to the British threat.

In Williamsburg, Rebecca penned a brief letter to James. She was not sure where to send it, but trusted it would find him eventually.

April 22, 1781

Dearest James,

The enemy departed the city this morning, marching toward Jamestown, where their fleet is. They left the barracks in ruins, as well as my uncle's sheds, but his house and outbuildings thankfully still stand. All in all, the city is relatively unscathed, including the Raleigh, which had to tolerate British officers for two nights. They apparently tried to pay for their rooms, but your mother refused to accept their money.

All of our sick fared well during the enemy's brief stay, and General Phillips even sent a doctor with some medicine to assist. I had another encounter with the traitor Arnold, who recognized me at the Palace. I suspect he was the one who burned the barracks, as he seems to get pleasure from such things.

We know little of your whereabouts, other than you marched off to New Kent. Please let me know how you are as soon as you can. And please find out how John fares. I have not heard from him in months. Until we meet again, I remain,

Your Loving and Affectionate,

Becca

In South Carolina, John encamped with the American Southern army. They were just outside of Camden, still under General Greene, who was eager for battle. Greene had marched his army back to South Carolina after the Battle of Guilford Courthouse in mid-March. It had taken them a month to travel one hundred and fifty miles, and Greene had expected General Cornwallis to follow him with the remnants of his army—about fifteen hundred men—but the British commander had not. He had stayed in Wilmington, North Carolina until late April, seemingly unsure how to proceed. General Greene was surprised yet relieved by Cornwallis's complacency, and sought to take advantage of it by attacking British outposts in South Carolina. His first target was Camden.

Before commencing his march to South Carolina, General Greene re-organized his army. A number of Virginia Continentals whose enlistments had expired, including most of the men from John's own company, were discharged and sent home, but John still had six months left on his enlistment, so he was placed in Captain Conway Oldham's company of Virginia Continentals. John was joined by Sergeant Collins and the few remaining men from his previous company.

John's new company was placed in one of the two Virginia Continental regiments still with General Greene's army. John's regimental commander was Colonel Richard Campbell, and like John's company commander, Captain Oldham, Colonel Campbell was an experienced officer. Both officers had stellar reputations among the men, and John considered himself fortunate to serve under them.

The two officers were not the only ones with a solid reputation, however. John discovered to his satisfaction that despite his youthful age of seventeen, he had *also* gained a positive reputation among the men in his new company. Somehow, stories of John's service at Cowpens, his rescue of Colonel Porterfield at Camden, and his escape from the Waxhaws Massacre the previous spring, had spread among the company and he was now seen as a veteran soldier, someone you could count on.

Some disbelieved the stories at first, thinking John was too young to have done so much, but Sergeant Collins confirmed them, and John's own behavior made it clear that he was indeed a veteran soldier. Elated at the development, John wrote to James about his elevated status in the company.

April 15, 1781

Dear James,

It has been months since I last heard from you. I trust you received my letter of January 30th that described Cowpens, but I imagine my letter of March 20th has yet to reach you.

Since that letter, we have been on the march back to South Carolina. I think General Greene's objective is to draw Cornwallis here, but I have heard nothing on that score.

Presently, we are not far from Camden, and I think we plan to attack the garrison there. I have been placed in a new company under Captain Conway Oldham. He is a veteran of the 12th Regiment and a fair man, but we all lament the loss of Captain Wallace. At the start of this month the bulk of his company were discharged, so I was transferred to Captain Oldham's company. Sergeant Collins, whom I have written about before, joined me, as did a few others, but everyone else from Captain Wallace's company has returned to Virginia.

My new company is attached to a regiment commanded by Lt. Col. Richard Campbell. He, like Captain Oldham, is from the Valley, and began his service under Muhlenberg with the 8th Virginia. I remain fortunate to serve under experienced officers who garner the respect of the men.

I know this will sound like boasting, but I've sensed a degree of respect from many of the men in my new company. Although I am still younger than most, I've been with the army for over a year now, and have seen many battles, including Cowpens, which seems to impress them. It helps that Sergeant Collins speaks of me highly, too. Most of the men are eighteen-month draftees who only just saw their first action at Guilford last month, so in their eyes, I am a tested veteran.

Miss Jenkins and her father joined us in camp after the battle at Guilford to help with the wounded. They continue with the army, but did not march here with us, as too many wounded from Guilford still needed their help. They will hopefully rejoin us here when they can. I am particularly fond of Miss Jenkins, James. The way you are fond of Becca.

How does Becca fare? I have not heard from her since last year, though I heard that the traitor Arnold attacked Richmond. I hope she didn't have the displeasure of encountering him. Though if she did, I pity Arnold. That glare she has can turn your blood cold! Please give her my warm regards, and do the same to our parents and siblings.

As you can see, I have run out of space, so must end this here. I wish you well, dear brother, and remain,

Your Most Affectionate,

John

General Greene's troops reached the outskirts of Camden four days after John wrote to James. The American commander was surprised to discover that the fortifications surrounding the town, and the thousand-man garrison defending it, were much stronger than expected. As a result, he tried to draw the enemy out to attack his force of twelve hundred fifty men (mostly Virginia, Maryland, and Delaware Continentals). Greene halted the army on Hobkirk's Hill, two miles north of Camden, set up camp, and waited.

On the morning of April 25th, several cannons arrived to bolster the army's firepower, but much more importantly to John, Abigail and her father arrived and rejoined the army. Their arrival was timely, for on that very day their services would be greatly needed.

John learned of their arrival from one of his tentmates, but before he got a chance to greet them, musket fire erupted in the woods to the left front of the army.

The British commander at Camden, Lord Francis Rawdon, had decided to surprise the Americans by leaving his earthworks and attacking Greene's left flank. As the British approached, however, they were discovered by American sentries who then fired upon them. Their musket shots alarmed the rest of the American army, who quickly formed for battle.

John was posted on the right flank of the American line, which bisected the road to Camden. The other Virginia regiment of Continentals, under Colonel Samuel Hawes, was posted to the left of John's regiment. Several cannons were posted in the road to the left of the Virginians, and on the other side of the road were two more Maryland regiments, and a company of Delaware Continentals. It was a strong line of troops, and John felt a confidence going into battle that he'd never felt before.

General Greene noticed that his line extended beyond both ends of the approaching enemy, so he ordered his two flank regiments to advance and wheel toward the enemy to envelop them from both sides. While those regiments swung left and right to strike the British, Greene's two center regiments advanced straight ahead.

John's confidence continued to soar as he and his fellow Virginians closed in on the enemy. *They've walked right into a trap,* he mused to himself, *and we'll bag the whole lot of them.*

Lord Rawlins realized his danger, however, and deployed his reserve, extending his line to match the

Americans and blunting Greene's attempt to envelop the British.

The battle was now a contest of nerves, and each side stood resolute as they blasted volley after volley at each other across the wooded terrain.

Much to John's disappointment and surprise, it was the Americans who backed down first.

One of the Maryland regiments on the left became disordered and confused and withdrew from the fight. The disorder spread to the other Maryland regiment, and soon the entire left side of General Greene's line was forced back.

Colonel Hawes and his Virginians initially held firm, but Colonel Campbell's regiment, in which John served, also began to retreat. Greene thus ordered the entire army to disengage from the fight and march north.

John was repulsed by the whole affair. "Why are we withdrawing?" he growled as they returned to the summit of the hill and continued down its other side. "They haven't beaten us!"

"Just do as you're told, lad," replied Sergeant Collins. "General Greene knows what he's doing."

Greene's army withdrew several miles to the north and halted when they determined that the British were not pursuing them. About thirty men from John's regiment had fallen in the battle—approximately two hundred seventy Americans were lost in all. The British suffered similar losses, but since they held the field, they were the victors.

When the Americans halted for the evening, John asked Lieutenant Deane if he could report to the hospital tent.

"Are you hurt, Mr. Southall?" Deane asked.

"No, sir. It's just Doctor Jenkins rejoined the army this morning and—"

"Did you mean *Miss* Jenkins?" the lieutenant chuckled, aware of John's feelings for her. John reddened and opened his mouth to protest, but Lieutenant Deane waved him off. "Say no more, lad," he grinned. "You may go."

The scene in the makeshift hospital tent was utter chaos, so much so that John thought about turning around and returning later, but then his eye caught Abigail's and she rushed over to check on him.

"Are you hurt, John?" she asked, her hands flailing about as she inspected his body.

“No, no, I’m fine. I haven’t a scratch.”

“Thank God,” she said, stepping back. There was a shout of agony in the distance and Abigail cringed, her head flitting back and forth between John and her duty. “I, um, I—”

“I know, I know,” interrupted John. “I’ll let you be and stop by later.”

Abigail smiled and kissed John on the cheek. “I’ll see you in a little while.” She then spun around and dashed off.

John returned to his company, which had set up tents with the rest of the army for the evening.

“No luck?” Lieutenant Deane called out to John when he spotted him.

John smiled and gave a small shrug. “She’s too busy to see me right now.”

With over a hundred wounded soldiers to treat and just a handful of doctors and nurses to do so, Abigail spent the remainder of the day—and much of the evening—at the hospital.

Captain Oldham learned of John’s request to visit the hospital and like Lieutenant Deane, understood why.

"You served in a hospital in Hillsborough, didn't you, Mr. Southall?" Captain Oldham started. "Why don't I detach you to serve in this one? At least for the time being."

John happily agreed with the proposal and reported straight to Abigail at 9 p.m.

"I'm sorry, John, it's just been impossible to—"

"Shhhh," he replied. "I've been detached here to help."

Abigail beamed, then called excitedly to her father, "John is back to help with the chamber pots!"

The army moved further north the next day, stopping at Rugley's Mill. John kept busy loading and unloading the wagons with wounded men and supplies.

General Greene remained at Rugley's Mill for two weeks, waiting on news of General Cornwallis, as well as British activity in South Carolina. With John assigned to hospital duty, he was able to see Abigail every day, and they continued to grow closer.

In early May, General Greene was relieved to learn that General Cornwallis had indeed marched north from Wilmington, North Carolina toward Virginia with his battered force of redcoats. Although he knew Cornwallis's decision was bad news for Virginia, it provided General Greene with the opportunity to strike at vulnerable British outposts in South Carolina without worrying that Cornwallis might suddenly show up.

Lord Rawdon in Camden recognized the vulnerability of his post and abandoned it on May 11th, withdrawing to Charleston.

"Without Cornwallis, they just don't have enough troops to hold all their outposts in this state," Greene speculated to his staff. "Now is the time to strike them."

Camden had been a key link in a chain of British outposts that arced across South Carolina's interior from Georgetown on the east coast, to Ninety-Six, an outpost near the Georgia border to the west. Greene knew that the loss of Camden weakened the other outposts—especially the smaller ones nearby—so he ordered Colonel Henry Lee and militia generals Francis Marion and Thomas Sumter to attack them.

Meanwhile, Greene marched his main army westward, toward Ninety-Six. John returned to Captain Oldham's company when the march to Ninety-Six began, while Doctor Jenkins and Abigail marched with the army's baggage and camp followers in the rear of the column.

While General Greene and his American Southern army went on the offensive in South Carolina, General Phillips and his British force of twenty-five hundred men continued their operations in Virginia. General Peter Muhlenberg had challenged Phillips at Petersburg, twenty miles south of Richmond, in late April, but Muhlenberg's one thousand militia had been far too few to stop the British.

After General Phillips had captured Petersburg, which was an important supply depot for the Virginians, Phillips marched his force north, toward Richmond.

Governor Jefferson and Virginia's legislators fled to Charlottesville upon news of the enemy's approach on Richmond. They left several hundred poorly armed militia under General Nelson, now fully recovered from his long illness, behind.

James continued to serve as General Nelson's aide and was discouraged at the size and condition of the militia. *We'll never be able to stop them,* he worried, as he looked over the morning troop reports. *We need more men.*

General Nelson held the same view and refused to waste his men's lives in a futile fight to protect Richmond.

So, he led the militia northward in hopes that reinforcements would soon join him.

To the delight of General Nelson and James, that is exactly what happened when General LaFayette arrived in Richmond on April 30th with a thousand Continental light infantry. These were the same troops General Washington had sent to Virginia in March. They had halted in Annapolis, Maryland, when the plan to capture Benedict Arnold in Portsmouth unraveled, and a disappointed General LaFayette had turned around to march back to New Jersey to rejoin Washington's army. General Washington, however, had ordered LaFayette to continue to Virginia and lead the resistance to the British there.

Although General Phillips still significantly outnumbered the combined American force of Continentals and militia in and around Richmond, he declined to attack. Instead, Phillips marched his army back to their ships at City Point, reboarded them, and set sail down the James River.

General LaFayette cautiously followed General Phillips by land as the British fleet slowly sailed down the river. LaFayette's militia grew to over one thousand men and were then formed into two brigades under General Nelson and General Muhlenberg, respectively.

James wrote to Rebecca in mid-May to describe the condition of the army and the impact LaFayette's arrival had had.

May 12, 1781

Dearest Becca,

We are currently encamped below Richmond on the north side of the river, watching the enemy, who seem uncertain how to proceed. A week ago, they sailed downriver, but then turned around and have returned to Petersburg.

General LaFayette, who continues to impress me with his fine character, thought they intended to march to North Carolina, but their long stay in Petersburg suggests they are waiting, and now there are reports that General Cornwallis is marching to Virginia. The great fear is that Cornwallis plans to unite with Phillips at Petersburg.

Our force is no match for Phillips, much less Cornwallis *and* Phillips, so I do not know what we will do if this happens.

While General LaFayette's Continental troops appear to be excellent soldiers, our militia pales in comparison—

especially since so many are unarmed and poorly dressed. General Nelson commands one of the two militia brigades, General Muhlenberg the other, and they total over twelve hundred men. We have some cavalry and cannons as well, but all told, our force is no match for the enemy.

Like you, I have not heard from John in months. General Greene has apparently returned to South Carolina, so I suspect that John has found little opportunity to write. I worry that none of our letters have found their way to him, nor his to us. I trust that he is safe, though, so please try not to worry too much.

Please convey my regards to your family, and give the same to my mother and siblings. My father remains with Colonel Innes, who I am told shall return to Williamsburg as a precaution against another enemy visit. Until we meet again, I remain,

Your Ever Obedient and Affectionate,

James

Unfortunately, the reports of Cornwallis's expected arrival proved true. He reached Petersburg on May 20th with fifteen hundred men and assumed command of all British forces in Virginia.

General Phillips had shockingly died from an illness a week earlier, leaving General Arnold briefly in command. Soon after Cornwallis's arrival in Petersburg, however, Arnold would return to Portsmouth and then sail to New York to report to the overall British commander in America, General Henry Clinton. Arnold's time in Virginia was over. General Cornwallis now directed British operations in Virginia, and before May's end, he would go on the offensive.

Chapter Twelve

Siege of Ninety-Six

Two days after General Cornwallis had reached Petersburg, General Greene arrived at the British outpost of Ninety-Six in South Carolina. He had just one thousand troops, mostly Continentals, fit for duty with him. Colonel Lee's Legion and the militia detached to him had yet to rejoin Greene.

Twelve hundred and fifty American loyalists, as good as any British regulars and outfitted in red coats, were defending the British post at Ninety-Six. They were commanded by Lieutenant-Colonel John Cruger of New York.

Cruger and his men were protected by a series of fortifications, beginning with a sturdy wooden wall of upright logs that surrounded the small village of Ninety-Six. Several buildings had been converted into fortified block houses, and a thick layer of abatis (sharp, entangled branches spread in front of a defensive position to slow an approaching enemy) surrounded the entire village.

Map of Ninety-Six

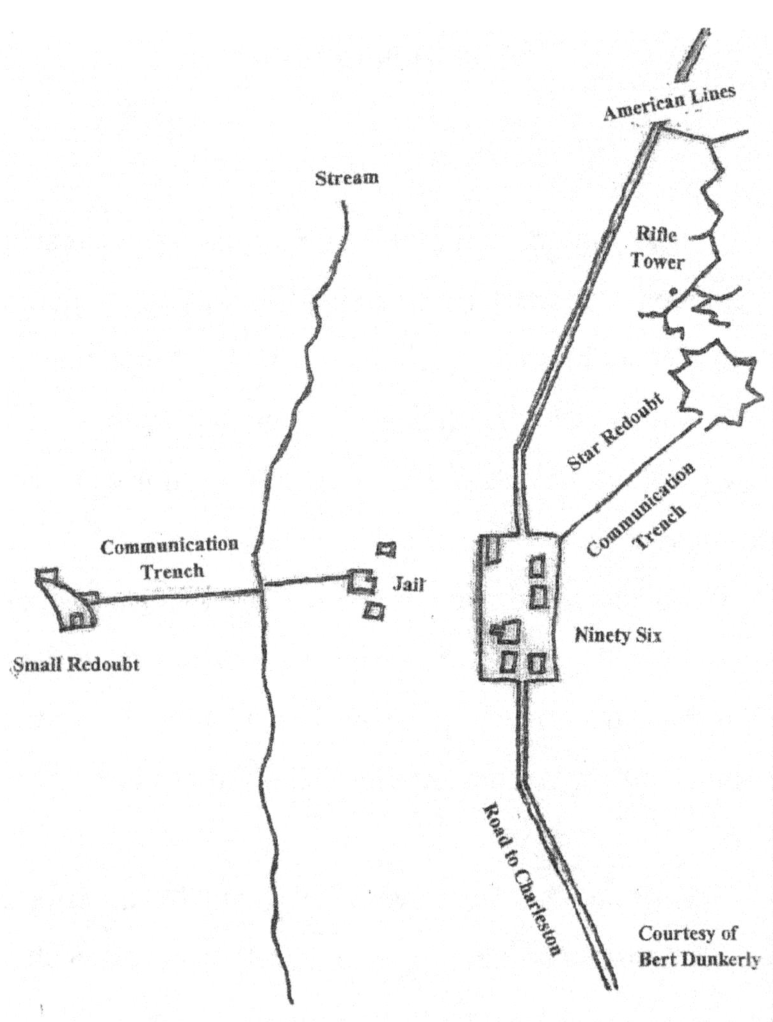

In addition, two strong forts (called redoubts), just east and west of the village, guarded the approach to Ninety-Six. If General Greene was to capture Ninety-Six, he had to first take control of at least one of these redoubts.

Greene focused his effort upon the redoubt east of the village, which he considered the most critical part of Cruger's defense. It held several hundred troops, four cannons, and was shaped like an eight-pointed star. The fort's thick fourteen-foot-high earthen walls protected its defenders from enemy fire and presented a difficult obstacle for the Americans to overcome.

But that wasn't all. Two additional obstacles were positioned outside the redoubt. Encircling the entire redoubt was an eight-foot-deep ditch, making scaling the fort's walls even more challenging, and to make things worse, a thick layer of tangled abatis was spread in front of the ditch. All of this would surely slow, perhaps even stop, the Americans.

General Greene had two options to attack the redoubt. He could try to storm it with a direct assault—which would be extremely costly for his men as they advanced over open ground, struggled through the abatis and ditch, and then up and over the wall, all while under deadly cannon and musket fire. It was not a great option.

Greene's other option, however, was to lay siege to the redoubt. This would involve digging a series of trenches toward the redoubt to protect his men from enemy fire. The problem, however, was that a siege would take *much* more time than a direct attack, and Greene wasn't sure he could complete a siege and capture Ninety-Six before British reinforcements arrived. Despite his concerns, Greene ultimately decided a siege was the better option.

John was relieved when rumors spread through the camp that General Greene had chosen to lay siege to the star redoubt. The thought of charging across the open field and into the obstacles outside the redoubt, all while under heavy enemy fire, had frightened him. *It would've been a blood bath,* he thought.

John had never participated in a siege before, he'd only read about them. Still, he knew that his chances of surviving a siege were much higher than a direct assault upon such a fortified position.

There was one man in the camp who had participated in a siege—Sergeant Thomas Digges. Digges was in John's regiment and had been at Savannah in 1779 when

American and French troops laid siege to the British there. With the rest of the men consumed with worry over the siege, Digges was peppered with questions in camp about what to expect.

"It's a lot of work, that's for sure," explained Sergeant Digges. "But I'd rather dig all day and night than charge across that open field against a fort like that."

"How long do you think it will take?" asked John.

Digges rubbed his chin. "That's hard to say," he said. "The ground is pretty hard. And there's no shade out there, so it's going to be hard on us. Not sure what we have for entrenching tools either."

"How does one even get started on such a massive task?" asked Joseph Wiggins, one of the most cynical soldiers in the regiment.

"Well, I can only tell you what we did at Savannah," replied Digges. "Before we started digging, we spent about a week building hundreds of gabions."

"A week!" cried Wiggins.

The others ignored him. "What are gabions?" asked a young soldier John did not know.

"They're big hollow baskets, three feet tall, woven from saplings and vines. We'll build a lot of those and take them out with us when we start to build our trenches."

"And just what are baskets going to do against cannon balls?" Wiggins scoffed.

"Nothing," confessed Sergeant Digges, "but I hadn't finished. We'll line the gabions side by side, along the point the engineers pick for our first parallel, and fill them as fast as possible with dirt."

"What!" cried Wiggins. "While we do that those baskets will be blasted to pieces, us with them!"

Sergeant Digges scowled at Wiggins, frustrated at his interruptions. "Son, if you'll let me finish, I'll explain why that won't happen."

The sergeant paused, as if to challenge Wiggins, daring him to speak. But Wiggins said nothing. He only crossed his arms and grunted. Sergeant Digges nodded at him. "Thank you," he said before he continued. "So, we don't go out there in daylight to start the parallel, that would be foolish. We go out under the cover of darkness. And if we do it right, if we fill those baskets and throw more dirt on and around them to boot, we'll have good cover from the enemy by dawn. Remember, the gabions are three feet high, but we're also digging a trench behind them that will be a couple of feet down. So by sunrise, we should have a good six-foot earthwork between us and the fort." The men exchanged glances around the fire, all of them unconvinced that they would really be protected.

Digges chuckled as he took in their skepticism. "Oh, they'll fire at us for sure once they discover us, but they won't be able to see us behind the earthwork so their shots will be random and wasted. Believe me."

John had tried his best to visualize everything, but was still struggling. "Why is the trench called a parallel?" he asked.

"I imagine because it is dug parallel to the enemy's works. The parallels are where we'll spend most of our time when we're not in camp."

"Where do you think we'll start the first one?" asked John.

"I'm not sure, that's General Greene's decision. We started the one at Savannah some six-hundred yards from the enemy's works."

"Six-hundred yards!" exclaimed Wiggins in protest, unable to stay silent any longer. "What good is a parallel six-hundred yards away from their fort? That's way out of range of our muskets. Why do all that digging for nothing? We'll be too far to be of any use!"

"This is just the starting point," Digges snapped, now thoroughly annoyed at Wiggins. "We'll use our first parallel to protect us, and then bring our cannons up to shell the fort while we dig new trenches out toward the enemy. Then we'll build a second parallel closer to them and do it all again, until we get right up close to their fort."

"I see what you mean about all the work," John groaned. "That's going to take *a lot* of digging."

"Yes, it's a lot of work, a hell of a lot of work. But it beats storming the works directly over that open field," replied Sergeant Digges. "At Savannah, we ran out of time and had to storm their earthworks." He shook his head and shivered, reflecting on the carnage that had occurred in the failed attack. "I'll take a siege any day over a direct assault of a fort."

Although Greene had decided upon a siege of the redoubt, he still worried that it might not be completed before British reinforcements from Charleston arrived to relieve Ninety-Six. "We can't let ourselves get caught between two enemy forces," Greene told his staff. "We must start as soon as we can *and* as close to the redoubt as possible."

John and the rest of Greene's army spent the next three days in camp building gabions as fast as they could. General Greene's sense of urgency led him to begin digging the first parallel on the evening of May 25th.

Under the cover of darkness, Greene's men crept unnoticed until they were within a hundred yards of the star redoubt, much closer than what was recommended by his engineers. The gabions they carried were placed in a row and quietly filled with dirt, providing cover for the men, just as Digges had said. In the morning, when the British troops in the star redoubt discovered the new American trench, they began a fierce bombardment of it.

Sergeant Digges, who had remained in camp with the rest of John's regiment, realized General Greene's mistake and explained it to John and his comrades.

"The first parallel is too close. It should be at least two hundred yards further back. Those men are isolated out there. The ground between them and us is wide open. We'll be slaughtered if we try to reinforce them in daylight. The first parallel should have been dug further back, out of range of the fort's muskets. We could easily reinforce it then, and dig new trenches toward the redoubt to build a second parallel. The general placed the first parallel where the third one ought to be."

Though everything Digges had told them prior had proved to be true, John did not want to believe he was right about this. He wanted to believe that General Greene had made the right call and hoped that Sergeant Digges was wrong. Unfortunately, he discovered otherwise in the early morning hours when fighting erupted at the first parallel.

A large enemy detachment from the redoubt had snuck up on the Americans and surprised them. Most of General Greene's men, who were focused on expanding the first parallel, fled in panic back to camp, leaving their entrenching tools behind. The loyalists happily retrieved these tools and returned to their redoubt with them, pleased that they had so easily routed the Americans.

General Greene recognized his mistake in placing the first parallel so close to the enemy and had no choice but to abandon it. A new parallel was begun the next evening, some four hundred yards from the star redoubt. Strong covering parties—which included John and his company—guarded the work detail against attack, and before dawn, a new first parallel was ready for use.

John rotated from the parallel to camp like everyone else. And just like everyone else, he hated it. The work was exhausting and never ending, and he found little time to visit Abigail, who kept busy treating mostly sick soldiers in the camp hospital.

Not surprisingly, John found his time in the trench harder than being back at camp, but that didn't make the work at camp feel any easier. John and his comrades spent countless hours making gabions for the siege. He described the progress of the siege to James during its second week.

June 8, 1781

Dear James,

Your letter of March 10th, finally reached me, but it appears that none of my letters have reached you since last year. As nearly three months have passed since your letter, I can only imagine much has changed in Virginia. In fact, we have heard reports that Cornwallis marched there and united with British reinforcements from New York, and that General LaFayette commands the American forces in Virginia.

We have been modestly successful this spring, forcing the enemy to abandon multiple forts here in South

Carolina. We are now encamped outside a strong village called Ninety-Six, and have commenced a siege of the place. The enemy are numerous and well-fortified, but we make steady progress against one of their forts outside of the village.

I rotate from the trenches to the camp spending one full day and night in the trenches and then two days in camp, but the days in camp are not meant for relaxing. We keep busy building gabions. The work of a siege is exhausting, brother. My hands are covered with blisters and cuts, but it is better than the alternative. A direct assault upon the fort would surely cost us a lot of men.

The evenings here are warm, but generally comfortable. The days, however, have become unbearably hot—especially since there is little shade for us. Summer seems to arrive a month earlier here than in Virginia.

If you were to see me James, I don't think you'd recognize me. My clothes, which are torn and ragged, hang off me now, and my hands and face are dark and rough like a fieldhand's. There is nothing glorious about this work, yet it must be done if we are to succeed.

But I need not tell you, an aide to General Nelson. I assume he has recovered and that you are with him and General LaFayette at headquarters, wherever that is.

How are Mother and Father? And Becca? I was surprised to learn in your letter that she had moved back to Williamsburg. Is it true that the British briefly occupied the city in April?

I am as much concerned about events in Virginia as I am here, as it seems the focus of the enemy has shifted there. Please write to me when you can to let me know how everyone is. Until then, I remain,

Your Obedient and Loving Brother,

John

The Star Redoubt and American Trenches

Chapter Thirteen

You Did Good, Lad, Real Good

John had good reason to be concerned about events in Virginia. In late May, General Cornwallis, confident of victory against LaFayette, had left Petersburg with over five thousand troops and crossed the James River.

General LaFayette, who had been near Richmond since the last day of April waiting for the British to act, suspected that Cornwallis's target was an important weapons foundry in Fredericksburg. Far too weak to engage the British in battle, LaFayette wisely kept his distance from Cornwallis and instead withdrew north as Cornwallis advanced on the road to Fredericksburg.

In actuality, the British commander was not interested in Fredericksburg. He merely wanted to destroy LaFayette's army. But General Cornwallis could not catch the Americans. To Cornwallis's ever-growing frustration, General LaFayette retreated each time the British approached.

Map of Central Virginia

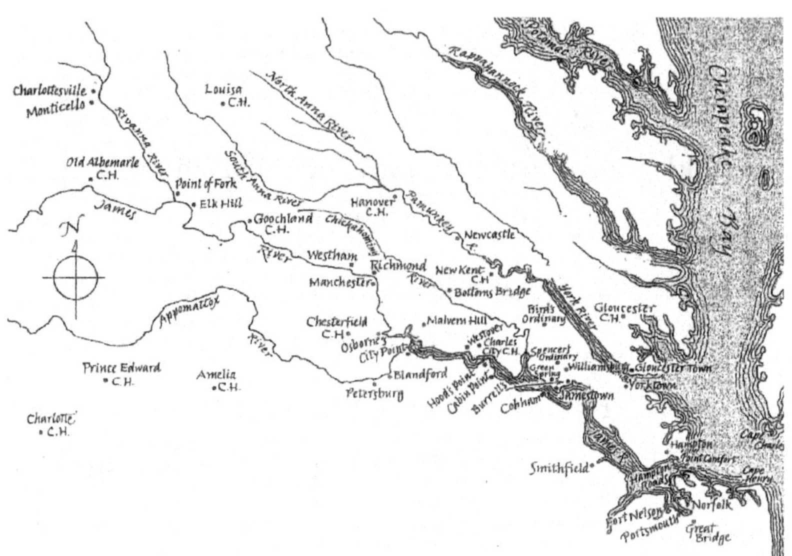

General Cornwallis's pursuit of LaFayette lasted a week, ending only when the British commander finally turned his attention westward in exasperation.

Cornwallis sent two large mounted detachments to the west ahead of his army. One, under Colonel Banastre Tarleton, was to strike the state Assembly—which had fled Richmond in April and reconvened sixty miles away in Charlottesville. Cornwallis's other cavalry detachment, under Colonel John Simcoe, was to attack an important American supply depot on the James River called Point of Fork. Five hundred newly raised Virginia Continentals were encamped there under General Steuben. He planned to send them to General Greene in South Carolina as soon as he could properly equip and clothe them.

When Simcoe's detachment drew close, Steuben—who believed his small force was no match for the British—abandoned Point of Fork without a fight, leaving valuable military supplies behind.

Colonel Tarleton's raid on Charlottesville, thankfully, was less successful. Most of the legislators were warned of his approach just hours before his arrival and thus were able to escape capture. They fled westward to Staunton, where the Assembly reconvened.

Tarleton and Simcoe rejoined General Cornwallis after their raids. Cornwallis still greatly desired to bring General LaFayette and his small army to battle, but the American commander continued to evade him.

LaFayette's small army grew by eight hundred men on June 8th, however, when General Anthony Wayne arrived with his Pennsylvania Continentals. General Washington had ordered them to join LaFayette, who had eagerly welcomed them into his army. Yet, even with reinforcements, the young Frenchman continued to keep his distance from the British army, which had turned its attention eastward toward Richmond.

On June 16th, a messenger from Staunton arrived in the American camp with stunning news. General Nelson had been elected governor by the state Assembly. Nelson prepared to ride to Staunton immediately and planned to bring James with him, but General LaFayette asked if James might remain and serve on his staff as a volunteer instead.

"I have long been impressed with the young gentleman and would benefit from his service to me," LaFayette told General Nelson. Nelson left the decision to James, who was honored by the request and agreed to stay.

James wrote to Rebecca to share the exciting news.

June 16, 1781

Dearest Becca,

It has been a very eventful two weeks, capped by a development today that I am still in shock over. We have marched continuously to stay out of Cornwallis's reach. We've been reinforced by eight hundred Pennsylvanians but are still too weak to challenge his army. So, Cornwallis runs rampant over the state. He's dispersed the Assembly in Charlottesville and looted a supply depot on the James River.

Yet, our army survives and remains a threat to him, hovering near his encampment at Elk Hill, waiting for an opportunity to strike. I think General LaFayette has played his hand very wisely, which makes the news I'm about to share all the more interesting.

General Nelson learned today that the Assembly in Staunton has chosen him to be governor. He asked me to attend to him, but General LaFayette requested that I stay with the army and serve on his staff as a volunteer. General Nelson left the decision to me and, being very flattered by General LaFayette's request, I felt compelled to remain.

So, I am now a volunteer aide-de-camp to General LaFayette, with the new rank of captain. As General Nelson has departed for Staunton, my duties for General LaFayette have already commenced.

I hope this news pleases you, especially since I forgot to wish you a happy 17th birthday last month. I apologize for that, but expect you understand why.

Please share the news with my parents and friends. I am quite proud of this honor and hope to be of real service to General LaFayette, who is indeed a fine leader. Until we meet again, I remain, as ever,

Your Most Affectionate and Loving Friend,

James

Meanwhile, in South Carolina, General Greene's siege of Ninety-Six progressed slowly. Greene had informed Congress on June 9th that, "Our poor Fellows are worn out with fatigue, being constantly on duty. The [enemy] works are strong and extensive. The position difficult to approach and the Ground extremely hard." Greene also reported that the British had been sending raiding parties from their fort against his trenches nearly every night, but, their very first raid aside, none had been successful.

Time was running out for General Greene and his men, however. Reports from Charleston claimed a British reinforcement was marching to relieve Ninety-Six. It was crucial that the siege be completed before this reinforcement arrived—else Greene's army would be caught between two enemy forces.

General Greene pushed his men hard and authorized several unorthodox efforts to overcome the enemy, including the construction of a tunnel from the second American parallel, and the construction of a thirty-foot wooden tower to fire down into the fort.

The tunnel failed completely. It never reached the ditch in front of the redoubt, but the riflemen who fired from the wooden tower had some success shooting into the fort until its defenders raised the height of their wall by stacking sand bags.

By June 18th, General Greene had run out of time. He either had to end the siege and withdraw, or storm the star fort and hope the rest of Ninety-Six would then fall. He chose the latter.

His plan was to attack the enemy from two sides early in the morning of the 19th. Colonel Lee would lead part of the army against the smaller British fort to the west of the village, while the main assault occurred from the third parallel, just thirty yards from the abatis in front of the star redoubt. Each was to storm the enemy position with a direct assault.

John was assigned to the lead element of the assault on the star redoubt. His detachment was called "the forlorn hope," because as the lead element, it was likely to suffer many casualties. Lieutenant Samual Seldon commanded the men, made up of twenty-five Virginians and a like number of Marylanders.

The rest of the army was to follow behind the forlorn hope, which was to charge through the enemy abatis, jump into the deep ditch, and then scramble up the steep embankment to punch a hole in the fort that the rest of the army could then flood into.

Lieutenant Seldon and his small detachment were in the third parallel before dawn. Some of the men carried long poles with hooks upon them to pull down the sandbags that the enemy had stacked recently.

As dawn's light began to flood the field, painting the horizon a garish red, John prayed. He prayed not for himself, but for Abigail, Rebecca, and his family. To his surprise, he was not afraid—at least, not as afraid as he thought he would be. His fear was overridden by a sense of pride. He and his comrades had toiled for months against the British, united under a vision of revolution, of freedom from Britain's reign. And it was this vision, this hope—a forlorn hope, perhaps—that fueled John forward.

The American attack was preceded by an artillery bombardment, which, unfortunately, did little damage. John and the others kept low in the third parallel and watched as artillery shells arced overhead toward the fort, their lit fuses streaking through the sky. The bang of an explosion followed, and John hoped it meant the enemy's defenses were damaged, or that some of the British had been killed or wounded. *The more damage the cannons cause, the easier the battle will be for us,* he reasoned.

There were several other blasts, and just as John began to wonder when the shelling would stop, it did.

"Let's go!" shouted Lieutenant Seldon, his sword raised. The brave American commander climbed out of the trench and dashed forward, straight into the enemy's abatis. Despite the cannon blasts, the abatis was still largely intact, which meant that John and his comrades had to struggle through it.

The branches tore at John's clothes and cut his skin, but he had no time to stop. If he stopped, he was as good as dead. *We have to get into that ditch,* he thought. *Move, move, move*!

The enemy was now firing from the top of the fort. Behind John, the main portion of the army waited for the forlorn hope to reach the redoubt. They fired over the heads of John and his comrades, trying to suppress the enemy's fire upon them. The riflemen posted in the thirty-foot wooden tower also fired into the fort, trying to further suppress the enemy and protect the forlorn hope.

John could see the ditch through the tangled branches, just feet away. He lunged forward, tearing through the branches that clawed at him. Finally, he reached the edge and slid down.

Lieutenant Seldon was already in the ditch, urging the rest of the men forward. "Up the bank, boys!" he cried before he scrambled forward.

It was a difficult climb up the steep embankment. The ground was soft and gave way, and for every two steps forward, it seemed like John slid back one.

The enemy gunfire from above was scattered. It was difficult for them to shoot into the ditch without exposing themselves to the American fire from the tower and third parallel. As shots rang out overhead, John scrambled upwards, slowly getting closer to the top.

Suddenly, he heard yelling below him. Some of the enemy had left the fort from the other side and circled around in the ditch, attacking the men still there. The British slammed into John's detachment on both flanks, prompting John and those around him to end their climb and slide down the embankment to join the brawl.

When John reached the bottom, he landed behind a loyalist who had just bayoneted an American. The American screamed, his hand clutching the wound as blood oozed through his fingers.

Enraged, John swung the butt of his musket around and clubbed the loyalist in the head. The dazed man collapsed, rolling to John's right. John thrust his bayonet forward into the man's side, a roar tearing through him. The man roared back in pain, but John, in a frenzy, pulled his musket back and bayoneted him again.

Out of the corner of his eye, John caught another loyalist coming at him, bayonet ready to strike. John whirled around, the loyalist's bayonet grazing his left side. But John did not feel the pain. He felt only rage as he swung his musket butt wildly at his attacker, clubbing him hard in the head. There was a sickening crunch of bone, and blood splattered across John's face as the loyalist dropped onto the embankment, unconscious.

At the base of the embankment, John noticed Lieutenant Seldon slumped over on the ground, his hands clutching his stomach. "It's hopeless," said the lieutenant. "Hopeless."

John wasn't sure if the lieutenant meant his wound or the attack, but he decided to get him out of there. John slung his musket over his shoulder and slid his hands under Lieutenant Seldon's armpits. He hoisted Lieutenant Seldon to his feet, then struggled to help him out of the deep ditch. John pushed him up the embankment from behind, and finally the lieutenant managed to drag himself over the edge and out of the ditch. John scrambled out after him, lifted the lieutenant to his feet once more, and the pair scuttled into the cover of abatis.

John felt Lieutenant Seldon go limp, unconscious from the loss of blood, but knew he couldn't stop. He struggled through the abatis, ignoring the searing pain in his hands as the branches sliced at him. Just as they reached the back edge of the twisted branches, with the third parallel just thirty-five yards away, John felt a thud upon the back of his left leg behind his knee. He collapsed to the ground as his knee exploded in pain.

Oh God, I've been shot, John realized as he lay still, Seldon motionless by his side. John craned his neck to try and see the wound, but everything was hazy. He thought back to Colonel Porterfield, who had suffered a similar wound at Camden. *He lost his leg. He lost his leg,* John thought in a panic. *Oh God, please don't let me lose mine.*

There was a dull roar in his ears, followed by a shrill whining, as the sounds of fighting faded away. Darkness encroached on the edges of his vision, and just as his eyes began to close, John felt a pair of hands grab him by his coat and drag him toward the American lines. As John fought to remain conscious, the sounds of battle returned. There was still plenty of shooting, but whoever had him pressed steadily on to the American trench.

Once they were safely away from the enemy, John was placed on a stretcher and brought back to camp. He passed in and out of consciousness during the journey and was fully unconscious by the time they reached the hospital tent.

The Struggle for the Star

Painting by Robert Wilson

When he awoke, Abigail was standing over him.

"You broke your promise, John," she said softly as he stared up at her, confused. "You went and got hurt again."

John shook his head, as if to clear his mind, and then it dawned on him. "How bad is it?" he croaked. "Did I lose the leg?" He tried to sit up to see, but Abigail placed a hand on his chest and eased him back down.

Her eyes softened as she said, "It's still there. But it's in pretty bad shape."

John let out a heavy breath. "As long as it's still attached." He grimaced as pain shot through him, and Abigail immediately offered her hand. He squeezed it, eyes clamped shut and teeth gritted as the wave passed through him. When it was over, Abigail's hand was red, but she did not remove it from his grasp.

She opened her mouth to say something, but John cut her off, his eyes wide with panic as a different thought seized him. "What of the attack?" he gasped.

"Don't worry about that now," Abigail replied, patting his hand.

But John needed to know. "What of the attack?" he asked again, his eyes hard.

There was a noise from the doorway, and both John and Abigail startled at it. Doctor Jenkins had arrived with Sergeant Collins, who had overheard John's inquiry. Sergeant Collins lowered his eyes and shook his head. "It failed, lad," he said quietly. "We're breaking camp and withdrawing."

John sunk back in his bed, a sense of failure descending upon him. "And what of Lieutenant Seldon?" he asked.

"He's here with you, son," responded Doctor Jenkins, a gentle smile on his face. "You got him out of the ditch."

Sergeant Collins leaned over to John and whispered, "You did good, lad. You did real good."

John smiled feebly, then drifted off into a deep sleep.

Chapter Fourteen

The British Return to Williamsburg

On the same day that James had been transferred to General LaFayette's staff, General Cornwallis had commenced a march to Richmond. LaFayette had pursued at a distance, still not ready to engage in battle despite his army having swelled to nearly four thousand men (eighteen hundred Continentals and over two thousand militia). That was still well short of the British, and LaFayette knew that the quality of Cornwallis's troops far surpassed his militia.

The other aides to General LaFayette had welcomed James into the general's family, which was another way to say staff. General LaFayette explained to James that he wished to use him primarily as a liaison with the militia, but also as an advisor or guide. "You did, after all, grow up in this region, did you not?" he asked James.

"I did, sir," James replied. "And I will eagerly assist you any way I can."

After pausing in Richmond for several days, Cornwallis continued to march east, toward Williamsburg. James grew more nervous with each mile, for he knew Rebecca was in Williamsburg and probably unaware that the British were approaching.

There was nothing LaFayette could do to stop Cornwallis, but he could harass the rear of the British army, which is exactly what he did on June 26th, when he sent a strong detachment of cavalry, light infantry, and riflemen ahead to tangle with Cornwallis's rear guard.

They clashed just six miles from Williamsburg, near Spencer's Tavern. The skirmish resulted in equal losses of thirty or so men on each side, and did nothing to stop Cornwallis from entering Williamsburg. But it did remind the British commander that the Americans were nearby and ready to strike.

Rebecca was at her uncle's home on Duke of Gloucester Street when the clash began in the morning. She heard the muffled gunfire, stepped out the front door, and saw a rider gallop by, yelling that the redcoats had returned.

She looked up the street toward the college and didn't see anything—at first. But then she heard the drums. She squinted and could barely make out the head of the British column coming down the street.

"Good Lord, they're back," she muttered to herself as she dashed into the house to warn her family.

Five thousand British troops—more than twice as many as in April—were marching into Williamsburg to occupy the former capital. Some were the same troops who had come in the spring, but most were not.

General Cornwallis turned Reverand Madison's home at the college into his headquarters and personal quarters, forcing the college president and his wife to take shelter in the main building.

Other officers also displaced families in town, sometimes allowing them to stay in one room of their home while other times, evicting them completely and forcing them to find shelter with family and friends elsewhere. The British army erected tents on the grounds of the college, on the Palace Green, next to the county courthouse, and outside of town, while the old Governor's Palace and its outbuildings were used as a hospital.

Rebecca stayed inside on the first day of the occupation, occasionally peeking out the window. She noticed redcoats, probably officers, enter the Raleigh

Tavern and worried about the Southalls. With so many troops in town, she expected a loud and boisterous evening, but it was surprisingly quiet.

The next day, she ventured to the market square with Sally, their enslaved cook, to buy some fresh produce. Only a handful of mostly empty carts were there, however, so the pickings were slim.

"We need to be careful with our food," Rebecca told her mother and aunt when she and Sally returned. She placed what she had obtained on the table; a few small carrots, a handful of potatoes, onions, and eggs, some dried fish, and a sack of corn meal.

"No ham?" asked Rebecca's aunt Hannah.

Rebecca shook her head. "I think the British are scooping everything they can up and leaving us with little."

Rebecca was correct. The British army was hungry and willing to pay for, or confiscate, whatever food they could find. The British *officers* were respectful and offered payment for the food, but some of the troops—and most of the British army's camp followers—gave no thought to payment. They took what they wanted and sneered at anyone who objected.

"It's best to stay indoors and avoid them," said Rebecca's mother, despite knowing that it was impossible to remain inside all hours of the day. "They can't stay forever."

On the fourth morning of the British occupation, the Andersons discovered that four of their enslaved people had run off, two from each family. "Cornwallis is apparently encouraging them to run," said Mrs. Anderson with disdain.

This was only partially true. General Cornwallis did not officially encourage or sanction the flight of enslaved people to his army, nor did he offer aid to those who fled. He did, however, look the other way and allow a growing number of runaway slaves to follow the army. Many received food from British officers whom they served.

Rebecca wrote to James on the sixth day of the occupation. She wasn't sure when she would be able to send the letter, and knew it was dangerous to write about the British while they were in Williamsburg, but she needed to vent her frustrations and share her thoughts.

July 1, 1781

Dearest James,

Williamsburg has been occupied by invaders for nearly a week. One cannot leave the house without encountering scores of them. They are encamped on most of the open spaces in town, have occupied every vacant building, and have even forced some people from their homes so they may use the property for their own quarters. Your parents' tavern is full of British officers who entertain late into each night. They seem very jovial and confident, although many of their men are poorly dressed.

There is also a very large number of camp followers with them, mostly wives and some children of the soldiers. Runaway slaves join their number daily. Many families, including ours and Aunt Hannah's, have lost people. Will and Kate left us the other night. They seem to think running to the British is their chance for freedom, but I fear it will end badly for them, as it did for Big John.

Our Virginia summer seems to have quite negatively affected the soldiers, and I am told the Palace is full of sick men. Part of me feels pity for them, but another part hopes their losses will drive them away. I heard today that some of the sick have smallpox, which has not plagued us for several years. I do not worry about catching it, but I do worry for your mother and siblings.

Do you have any news about Father? What of your father? I assume they are both with you in the army. And what of John? We have heard very little from the south lately.

Rebecca paused her letter here. Three days later she added to it.

July 4

It is a somber anniversary here, no one has dared acknowledge it for fear of catching the enemy's wrath, but we have some hope. It appears the invaders are preparing to leave. They have struck their tents and recalled their troops from the outskirts. Where they are going is not known, but we will all be relieved when they are gone.

Not only did they bring illness, but also hordes of flies that make it impossible to stay outside for very long. They've stolen many horses on their march, and I think they are the reason for the flies—although the army itself reeks of unwashed men.

6 p.m.

I just learned that some of them have marched for Jamestown, and the rest are expected to march by morning. It is believed they intend to cross the river there and continue to Portsmouth. Good riddance! Mother says at least they did not burn the town and destroy our buildings, and that may be true, but they did steal scores of slaves *and* brought disease with them.

I will try to send this once I am sure they have left and it is safe. Please give my love to Father, and my regards to your father.

Your Loving,

Becca

James was twenty miles away, near New Kent Courthouse, when Rebecca finished her letter. General LaFayette was aware of Cornwallis's movement to Jamestown and was making plans to draw closer to him. If Cornwallis was to cross the river, the rear portion of his force would be vulnerable while it waited to cross, making it an easy target.

On July 6th, LaFayette ordered General Wayne to lead an advance corps of his Pennsylvania Continentals—

joined by a detachment of riflemen, light infantry, and cavalry—toward Green Spring, six miles outside of Williamsburg. Green Spring was the former estate of William Berkeley, a royal governor from the previous century. James, who had visited the area several times with his father over the years, was ordered to join General Wayne as a guide.

General Cornwallis, however, had suspected that LaFayette might attack his rear guard, so he'd set a trap. He sent his baggage and some of his cavalry across the river, but hid the bulk of his five-thousand-man army along the wooded shoreline and posted a rear guard of several hundred men along the road from the ferry crossing to Green Spring, the direction from which Cornwallis believed the Americans would travel.

LaFayette was indeed determined to strike, and ordered General Wayne to march toward the ferry crossing with his advance guard. Wayne sent a battalion of Pennsylvania Continentals, one hundred fifty militia riflemen, a company of light infantry, and fifty cavalry—all together five hundred men—forward to scout the area. Wayne's men engaged the British rear guard, who were deployed in thick woods, and slowly pushed them back.

About an hour into the skirmish, General Wayne led his other two Pennsylvania battalions forward to support his advance troops. James rode alongside General Wayne, who appeared calm and confident.

James was less so. He had two years of experience with the militia, but had seen only brief battles. The alarms of 1779 and 1780 never amounted to any fighting, and the battle in Richmond with Arnold had ended almost as quickly as it had begun. True, things had gotten a little heated in that fight, but the militia had been swept aside so fast that it hardly seemed like a battle.

This situation was far more serious and far more dangerous. As a captain, James wore a sword, but to him it was merely a prop. He didn't have the slightest idea how to use it in battle. He only used it to point at things, or waved it around to get attention.

"Their men wouldn't resist this hard if they weren't trying to protect the remnants of the army," Wayne said to James, interrupting his thoughts as they rode forward. "I think we've caught the tail end of Cornwallis's army."

The reality of the situation, however, soon revealed itself. General Wayne's riflemen discovered Cornwallis's trap when they pushed the British guards into an open field. They paused, watched the redcoats scurry across it, then noticed on the opposite wood line, some three hundred yards away, thousands of British troops.

Wayne's advance guard had fallen right into Cornwallis's trap. The British commander ordered all his troops forward, and to their credit, the shocked Virginia riflemen halted, but did not run. They instead deployed in and around a farmhouse and some outbuildings, and began firing at the oncoming British.

The 1st Pennsylvania battalion under Colonel Walter Stewart came up next, and was also shocked at what they found. The Pennsylvanians deployed to the left of the riflemen, blocking the road. General Wayne, accompanied by James and another aide, rode up soon after and were equally stunned at the scene before them.

"My God!" cried James.

General Wayne turned in his saddle and yelled to the two battalions behind him. "Pennsylvanians! Advance and deploy on the center!" The two Pennsylvania battalions trotted forward and deployed on both sides of Colonel Stewart's battalion.

About one thousand Americans now faced off against *five* thousand British soldiers, who were advancing quickly upon them. James sat horrified next to General Wayne, waiting for his command. Wayne spurred his horse forward, turned to his men with his sword lifted and yelled, "Pennsylvanians, forward march!" He then swung his horse around to face the enemy and led the advance.

Is he crazy? thought James. *We're outnumbered five to one! This is suicide.* Yet, James rode alongside Wayne, his sword drawn and pointed forward, too.

James was not the only one questioning General Wayne's actions. General Cornwallis could not understand the rashness of his counterpart. *He's outflanked and outnumbered! Why is he advancing?* thought the British commander.

Wayne's nonsensical act caused Cornwallis to halt his own advance. *There may be more to this than I realize,* Cornwallis panicked, trying to figure if he had overlooked something.

The halt was exactly what Wayne had hoped for. He stopped his men as well, rode to the side, and yelled, "Battalion commanders, fire by company!" There was a brief pause as each commander gave the order to fire. Then an explosion of musketry erupted as the Pennsylvanians fired volleys into the British ranks, now less than a hundred yards away.

This rid Cornwallis of his doubt. He turned to an aide and said, "Advance the army, Captain," and the British captain shouted for the army to advance. When they had closed to about sixty yards, they halted and fired their first volley into the American ranks.

Musket balls whizzed past James and he struggled to control Spartan, who was spooked by all the noise. The Americans held their ground for what seemed like an eternity, but was really just three minutes. Then, General Wayne ordered a retreat. He turned to James and said, "Captain Southall, tell Colonel Stewart he must hold until the others withdraw."

James rode hard to Colonel Stewart, who was riding back and forth behind his men, encouraging them to hold their ground and keep up their fire. Stewart simply nodded when given the order and James galloped back to General Wayne.

The other battalions withdrew down the road in some disorder, riflemen mingled in among them. Stewart's battalion stood firm for just a minute, holding the road. Then, with the enemy advancing upon them from three sides with charged bayonets, they broke and fled to the rear, too.

It was now a race to escape, and though he wished to gallop away at top speed, James kept pace with General Wayne, who followed behind his fleeing troops, encouraging them to keep order.

I'm going to get shot in the back, James worried, as they rode on. *We're easy targets.*

But the firing behind them ceased, as did the British pursuit. Having successfully lured the Americans into a trap, Cornwallis mysteriously did not press his advantage. "It's too late in the day to continue," Cornwallis explained to an officer who'd asked if he should have Colonel Tarleton pursue them. "We've punished them enough."

American losses at Green Spring were around one hundred fifty men killed, wounded and captured. British losses were only half that.

It could have been much worse, thought James when he saw the troops return with the number of casualties listed. *We could have been destroyed.*

The British completed their withdrawal across the river the following day and marched on to Portsmouth, where they would stay for a month while General Cornwallis pondered his next move.

Battle of Green Spring

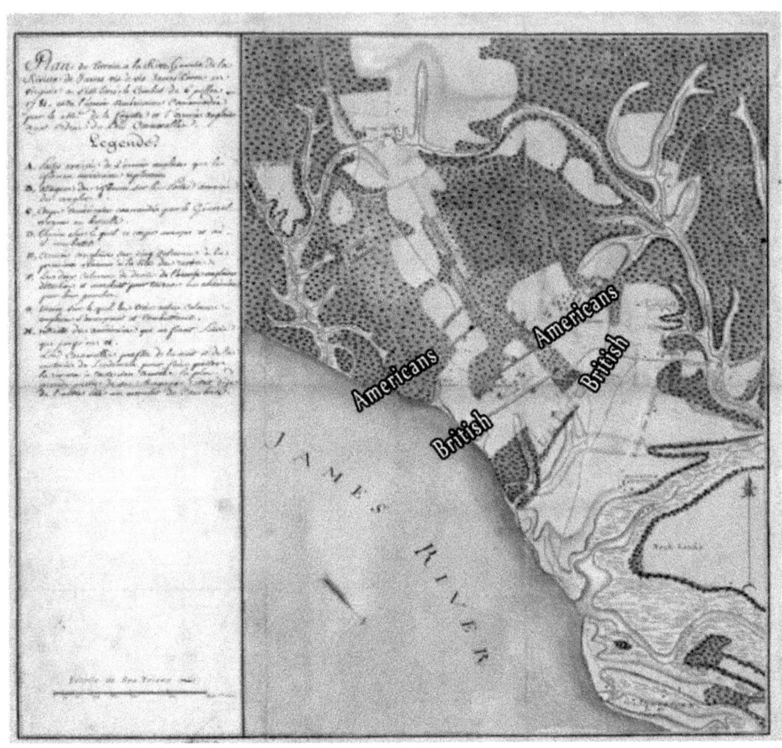

Chapter Fifteen

Overcoming Adversity

John awoke with a start in the back of a wagon next to another wounded, unconscious soldier. He was confused for a moment, unsure where he was or what was happening. The wagon bumped hard and jostled the last bit of sleep from him.

Oh, the attack, he thought. *My leg*. He reached down to check his leg but could only feel the edge of bandages and his thigh. *Did they take it?* he panicked, his earlier conversation with Abigail completely forgotten.

He lifted his head just enough to glimpse his left foot, still next to his right foot. *Thank God, it's still there*.
But then he felt the pain—a throbbing, burning sensation all around his left knee.

What happened? What happened? he wondered, trying to remember the attack.

He could remember most of it, even his struggle to get Lieutenant Seldon out of the ditch, but once he had done so, he could remember nothing else.

When the wagon stopped, he heard someone climb aboard and Abigail's smiling face appeared. "Well, hello," she whispered. "How do you feel?"

John tried to smile at her, but the pain contorted it into a grimace. "My leg and side hurts," he said.

Abigail placed a tender hand on his shoulder. "I'm not surprised, you were shot *and* stabbed."

John recoiled as the memory reared its ugly head. The fury he'd felt in the ditch surprised him, but it was the look on the face of the man he bayoneted—when he stabbed him a second time—that stuck in John's head. It was a look of terror, pleading, questioning; as if he were asking, "why did you do this to me?" That second strike had been a death sentence. John had known that—the poor soldier had known that. And that was what he saw in the man's eyes, the terrifying certainty that death was coming for him. It was awful. John shook his head, trying to rid himself of the image. *It was him or me,* he assured himself, then brought his gaze back to Abigail.

"How bad are my wounds?"

"The cut on your side isn't too bad. You were lucky. The bayonet really just scraped you. Though it may sting for a while." He waited for her to mention his leg, but

Abigail said nothing. When the silence stretched on, John knew the news wouldn't be good. He would have to pry it out of her.

John braced himself. "And my leg?" he forced out.

Abigail looked down, still not wanting to answer.

"And my leg?" John repeated a bit louder.

Abigail let out a long breath. "Father almost took your leg, John. And he still worries that he should have. The ball struck part of your knee."

"But he didn't, and it will heal—right?" John said, almost pleading with Abigail to agree.

Tears welled up in Abigail's eyes as she prepared to answer. "It will heal to a degree, but you'll never be able to walk or run like you used to. You'll have a limp, and need a cane for the rest of your life."

John felt like he'd been punched in the gut. "W-What?"

"You're crippled, John. Your wound is too severe."

John stared up at the sky, thinking, *No, she's wrong. I'll be alright.*

"The important thing is that you're alive. And you're going to keep living."

John smiled at her feebly, wishing she would leave. He needed to be alone. “I’m pretty tired,” he said. “Think I’ll try to sleep some more.”

Abigail stiffened, unsure if leaving him to sit with such news was the right thing to do. But finally, she nodded. “I’ll check on you again when we stop for the night,” she said, climbing down from the wagon and out of sight.

John stared up at the sky. He took a deep breath and then flexed his left foot. A pain so sharp it nearly stole his consciousness swept over him almost immediately. Tears welled as he stared at his bandaged leg. *Why, why, why?* he thought. He clenched his fists and took another breath. *They’re wrong, I’ll be alright. I just need time.* He flexed once more. A scream erupted from his throat, freeing the tears from his eyes. John let them fall, not caring who saw.

When the army stopped for the evening, John was lifted out of the wagon on a stretcher. He needed to go to the bathroom, but he couldn’t stand or sit, and didn’t know what to do, much less what to say. All of his clothes had been removed except his shirt, which extended down to his thighs.

This is so humiliating, he fumed, trying to build up the courage to ask for help. But then Doctor Jenkins arrived to check on him.

"How are you, son?" he asked.

John, who was laying on the ground on his stretcher, motioned for the doctor to come nearer.

"I have to relieve myself," he whispered, as if it were the biggest secret in the world.

Doctor Jenkins, who had bent over to hear, stood upright with a smile and said, "Of course, son. Of course." He turned and called two men over. "Take the lad over there," he said, pointing to some nearby bushes, "and help him with his business."

The orderlies lifted John up in the stretcher, took him to the brush, then helped him stand and held him while he did what he needed to do.

Is this what it's going to be like for the rest of my life? he wondered, ashamed of his helplessness.

When they returned from the brush, Abigail was there. John was glad she hadn't seen what had transpired. Two boxes had been removed from the wagon, and the stretcher now sat atop them, making it easier for Doctor Jenkins to examine John's wounds.

Doctor Jenkins removed the bandage on John's knee and inspected the wound closely, poking and pressing it with his fingers. *He looks concerned,* thought John. *He still wants to take the leg.*

The doctor caught John staring at him and said, "It looks better than I expected, son. But it's still pretty bad. I don't know how much function you'll have. We'll learn that over time. Right now, the most important thing is to keep infection away."

The doctor poured something on the wound that stung, and Abigail dabbed it dry. She then rebandaged the knee, which ached something fierce.

"Let's look at your side," Doctor Jenkins said. Abigail stepped behind John and placed her hands under his shoulders to help him sit up. She held him steady while her father removed the bandage that was wrapped around John's torso.

"Ah, this looks good," the doctor said, pleased that there was no redness or other signs of infection around the puncture wound just above John's hip. "They didn't hit anything important, and in a couple of weeks you won't even be able to tell that you'd been stabbed."

John smiled in relief as Abigail patted his shoulder.

“You need to rest some more,” Doctor Jenkins continued. “Tomorrow, we’ll get you up on your good leg and see how that goes.”

John nodded and Abigail eased him back down on the stretcher. “See,” she whispered in his ear, “you’re going to be fine. You’ll heal just fine.”

John smiled at her, thankful for her encouragement. But he wasn’t sure. If healing meant hobbling along, depending on others for the rest of his life, he wasn’t sure he *wanted* to heal. A life of dependency was not a life he wished to have.

The American army continued its march the next day and for several days after that. Finally, they stopped in an area of South Carolina called the High Hills. It was now late June, and the heat of the summer bore down on both armies, ending active campaigning for the time being. Each side sought to escape the heat and wait for cooler weather to resume operations.

The British abandoned Ninety-Six just a week after the siege had ended, and now concentrated their forces in and around Charleston. Those in the city or on the coast benefitted from the ocean breeze that occasionally blew inland.

General Greene encamped his army on wooded high ground along the Santee River, several days march from Charleston.

John luckily avoided infection in his wounds and began to heal slowly. By mid-July, he could walk short distances with the help of a cane, and with each passing day, he grew more and more hopeful that he might make a full recovery. Abigail and her father smiled uncomfortably when he suggested it, but didn't discourage him.

Before July's end, Doctor Jenkins approached John to talk, his face somber. "Abigail and I are returning to Hillsborough, son. We're not needed here at the moment, and I worry about her in these conditions."

The conditions he referred to included a shortage of food—particularly meat—which had led to many soldiers eating frogs, and sometimes alligators. It was the inactivity and brutal heat, however, that ultimately convinced the doctor to leave. Men still grew sick, but there were other doctors with the army who could tend to them. Doctor Jenkins and Abigail simply weren't needed, and likely wouldn't be needed again until the next fight, which looked to be many weeks away.

"I have to do what is best for Abigail," explained the doctor. There was a long pause before he added, "And we want you to come with us."

John was thrilled at the proposal. The thought of Abigail leaving crushed him—especially since he was now no use to the army, and therefore could no longer use military service to distract him from the loss he'd feel from her absence.

"It would please me immensely to go with you," John replied.

"Good then," responded the doctor. "I will speak to Colonel Campbell about your discharge."

John, Abigail, and Doctor Jenkins departed at the end of July. Before they left camp, Sergeant Collins came to say goodbye. He had with him John's discharge, signed by Captain Oldham.

"The captain sends his best wishes, lad, and so does the colonel. Here's your discharge, you're finished with the army." Sergeant Collins smiled awkwardly as he handed the document to John. "You're a fine soldier, lad. A real fine soldier. I'm going to miss you," he continued, a slight crack in his voice.

John's eyes watered, moved by Sergeant Collins's unusual show of emotion. "Thank you, Sergeant," he choked out. "Thank you for looking after me. I will always be in your debt."

Now Sergeant Collins's eyes grew misty. He extended his hand to John, struggling to speak. "We're going to miss you, lad," he said, his grip firm before finally pulling away. "Yes, sir, you're a fine soldier."

Abigail watched the exchange with misty eyes as well. Once they started on their way to Hillsborough she asked John, "How did you find out?"

"Find out what?"

"That it was Sergeant Collins that dragged you back to the trench."

John's mouth opened in shock. "I-I didn't—until now." He cast his eyes upwards. "I wish I'd known. He looked back toward the fading camp. "I would have said something."

"I thought you did. You said you were indebted to him."

“That’s because he always looked out for me. But he looked out for everyone in the company.” John’s voice cracked as he swiped at his tears. “Oh, I wish I had known.”

Abigail rested a hand on his shoulder, squeezing gently. “He knows how much you care for him. That’s what matters.”

John could only nod, tears trailing down his cheeks as he watched the camp fade further and further away.

Before their departure, John had written to James to update his brother on his situation. He told James that he was going to Hillsborough to recover, and that he could write to him there. Colonel Campbell had taken John’s letter and sent it north with his own letters and other army dispatches intended for Richmond.

It took two weeks for John, Abigail, and Doctor Jenkins to reach Hillsborough. They were all relieved that the journey was over, and were warmly welcomed home by the doctor’s neighbors. Doctor Jenkins converted his downstairs parlor into a bedchamber for John, and it took no time at all for John to settle into a routine of exercising his damaged leg.

And for the first time since he'd received news of his leg, John felt hope. *It's going to be all right,* he thought to himself one late afternoon as he walked with Abigail, arm in arm.

The situation had calmed considerably after the battle of Green Spring. General Cornwallis and his army spent the rest of July sweltering in Portsmouth, while General LaFayette and his troops waited along the James River for the British commander to act.

James wrote to Rebecca a few days after the Green Spring battle. The first half of his letter described the battle. The second half, written two days after he started the letter, described his service to General LaFayette—something he knew Rebecca was curious about.

July 10
The General has two aides who have been with him for some time and manage most of his correspondence. My function is primarily to offer advice about the militia and the state, particularly the terrain and the people that live here. I also deliver a lot of messages to officers and wait for their replies.

General LaFayette is a very careful and considerate commander whose politeness is exceeded by none. He uses charm to deliver unpleasant messages, which are often received with a smile by the recipient because of the flattery that accompanies the message.

Yet, he is also firm with the officers, some of whom are more than twice his age, and he is determined to preserve this army at all costs. I respect and admire him greatly, especially when I recall that he has voluntarily left his life as a French nobleman to join us here. There are few men like him, Becca, and it is an honor to serve on his staff.

As you can see, I have run out of space and must conclude. Please remember that I remain,

Your Most Loving and Affectionate,

James

Rebecca received the letter on the last day of July, when her father, who had briefly left the army in late July to check on his family, returned to Williamsburg. His stay was cut short, however, when a report from Yorktown arrived announcing that British troops had landed there. Major Anderson declared that he had to return to the army immediately.

Rebecca had meant to write back to James as soon as his letter arrived, but she'd been forced to put it off and now with her father's impending departure, she only had time to write him a brief note.

August 3, 1781

Dearest James,

Your description of the fighting at Green Spring was frightening. I am so relieved you escaped unharmed. I hope that in the future you can remain with General LaFayette, and that you don't go riding off into the thick of another battle.

Father is returning to you today, so I have taken the opportunity to write. Several reports have arrived in town that the British have landed at Yorktown. We do not fear them returning here, but expect that they may send parties to visit us from time to time. Why they have landed at Yorktown is a mystery, but of course, most of what they've done this year has mystified us.

I have not heard from John for some time. If you have, please write and let me know how he is. Until we meet again, remember that I am, and always will be,

Your Most Loving and Affectionate,

Becca

When Rebecca wrote to James, she was not aware that the entire British army in Portsmouth was moving to Yorktown. She assumed that the British troops that had landed at Yorktown were just a raiding party. But in fact, General Cornwallis had abandoned Portsmouth in favor of a new post, Yorktown. His intention became apparent to everyone within a week.

Like the situation in South Carolina, Virginia's oppressive summer heat suppressed military activities on both sides. The British slowly built fortifications around Yorktown, relying on the many runaway slaves who had fled to them to do much of the work. Meanwhile, General LaFayette moved his army from the James River to the Pamunkey River, which fed into the York River. This placed him in better position to observe and react to Cornwallis if need be. But then, in late August, General LaFayette received a letter from General Washington that changed everything.

A large French fleet was sailing to the Chesapeake Bay, and would arrive shortly. In addition, portions of the French and American armies to the north were marching to Virginia, commanded by General Jean-Baptiste

Rochambeau and General Washington himself. The plan was to trap Cornwallis in Yorktown, but to do so, General LaFayette had to keep the British there.

LaFayette summoned his division commanders to his quarters to explain the situation. James was present when the general revealed that, "General Washington and General Rochambeau are coming to Virginia with parts of their armies."

The officers assembled were stunned and elated by the news, unable to suppress their excitement.

"General Washington hopes to trap Cornwallis in Yorktown, so we must do what we can to keep him there. General Wayne, you will cross the James River with your Pennsylvanians and position yourself to block Cornwallis, should he attempt to return to the Carolinas. I will move the rest of the army to Williamsburg, to better observe them and attack should he try to escape to the James River. I expect that once His Excellency and General Rochambeau arrive with reinforcements, we will all march on Yorktown to lay siege to the enemy. Gentlemen, you have your orders."

James was thrilled by the news. After months of frustration at their inability to challenge Cornwallis, the Americans were going to turn the tables on him and take the offensive. James knew he shouldn't, but he had to write to John with the news. His letter was brief and cryptic, and he wasn't sure John would understand, but he wrote it anyway.

August 22, 1781

Dear John,

Much has happened in the past few days that would excite you. Our friends whom we have so long complained of are finally coming, as is the gentleman who introduced you to sweet bread. The enemy sits in Yorktown, content to stay for a long time, but we'll see about that.

I was heartily grieved to learn of your wound, but relieved to know you kept your leg. If anyone can recover from such a wound, it is you, John.

I have not seen Becca for some time, but she writes often and is well, as are our parents and siblings.

May you continue to recover and join us soon. I remain,

Your Affectionate Brother,

James

John received the letter on September 6th and immediately understood its meaning. “The French and General Washington are marching to Yorktown!” he announced. “I must return there as soon as I can.”

Doctor Jenkins and Abigail didn’t know how to respond. “How do you know this?” Doctor Jenkins asked, skeptical of the report.

“My brother’s letter,” John replied, waving it in the air. “He doesn’t come out and say it, but it’s there, trust me. General Washington is marching to Yorktown.”

The doctor paused for a moment before he announced, a glint in his eye, “Then we shall go and join him.”

Chapter Sixteen

Reunion

General Washington's plan to trap Cornwallis in Yorktown depended on several factors. Perhaps the most important was for the French navy to seize control of the Chesapeake Bay. The York River, upon which the town of York lay, flowed into the Chesapeake, which in turn, flowed into the Atlantic Ocean. As long as British ships could sail to Yorktown via the Chesapeake Bay, Cornwallis had a supply line and escape route at his disposal.

But if the French navy could block the York River or better yet, seize control of the entrance to the Chesapeake Bay, then the British supply line would be severed.

Two powerful French fleets converged on Virginia in late August to try and do this. They brought with them thousands of French troops, dozens of large siege cannons, and numerous warships to take control of the Chesapeake.

Admiral Francois Joseph Paul de Grasse commanded the French navy and sent his transport ships up the James River in early September to unload the three thousand troops he'd brought from the Caribbean. They marched to Williamsburg and encamped just west of the college. General LaFayette also marched his army to Williamsburg, arriving just ahead of the French.

James was glad to be back home in Williamsburg and was eager to see Rebecca, but his responsibilities prevented him from doing so. Things were simply too busy the day of their arrival.

Admiral de Grasse's warships remained in the Chesapeake, guarding the entrance between Cape Charles and Cape Henry. As expected, a large British fleet soon arrived to seize control of the Chesapeake from the French.

The naval clash that ensued off Virginia's coast on September 5th, was initially inconclusive. Both fleets suffered damage, but neither gained a clear advantage over the other. Several days of uncertainty passed as the two fleets maneuvered around each other. Then, shockingly, the British fleet disengaged and sailed back to New York for repairs. Thus, the French remained in control of the Chesapeake Bay, blockading General Cornwallis and his army in Yorktown.

Although Cornwallis no longer had access to the sea, the British army in Yorktown could still possibly escape by land. They would have to contend with General LaFayette's army and the three thousand French troops who had recently arrived in Virginia, which would be difficult, but the possibility remained.

Cornwallis, however, did not see the need to leave Yorktown. He believed the British navy would soon return to chase the French navy away and land reinforcements for his army. Cornwallis intended to keep Yorktown, so he directed his efforts in September to strengthening the defenses around the town.

Cornwallis set his men—and many of the enslaved men who had joined him over the summer—to work strengthening the earthworks and redoubts around Yorktown and the roads approaching it.

Back in Williamsburg, General LaFayette took quarters in the college and chuckled when James told him he had lived there for several years as a student. "I trust you were an excellent scholar," replied the general, "and that it was time well spent."

"Indeed, it was, General," replied James.

General LaFayette's aides shared a room next to his bedchamber. They knew that James was from

Williamsburg, and the next day brought the topic up in the presence of LaFayette, hoping the general would allow James a short reprieve to visit his family.

"Your family is still here?" the general asked when he overheard the boys talking.

"Yes, sir," said James. "They own a tavern on the other side of town."

"Well, you must go see them immediately, Captain."

James grinned at General LaFayette and his fellow aides, nodding to them in appreciation. His first stop was not the Raleigh, however, but to Rebecca's uncle's house. Rebecca leapt into his arms as soon as she saw him.

"You're back!" she exclaimed, forgetting all social graces and hugging him tightly.

"I've missed you," he replied, hugging her back.

When they separated, James acknowledged Mrs. Anderson, Hope, and the others in the house. They invited him to sit, but he said he had to visit his mother.

"I'll come with you," Rebecca gushed, grabbing her hat.

They hurried out the door and had a pleasant reunion with his mother and siblings, who asked repeatedly if James had any news about John.

"The last I heard, he was in Hillsborough, recovering from a wound in his leg. I think he is done with the army."

Mrs. Southall smiled uncomfortably, relieved that John was out of danger, but concerned about his wound. She did not want to sour the mood, however, so kept her focus on her oldest son. "Your father was here last night and said you were with General LaFayette," she said. "I'm surprised you could get away to visit, but oh so glad you did."

"Only briefly, Mother. There is much to do and I must return." James patted his younger siblings on the head, offering each a loving smile, before turning for the door.

Rebecca bid his family farewell and followed after him. "Where are you staying?" she asked.

"The college," James replied.

"Then I shall walk with you."

James was happy for her company, although it concerned him that she would have to walk home alone with several thousand troops, both American and French, about. General LaFayette had issued orders for the army to remain in camp, but numerous officers wandered off to visit the town.

To ensure Rebecca avoided the troops as best as possible, James proposed they walk together up to the church, and then part. Rebecca walked much slower than usual, which made James chuckle. He knew she did not want him to leave—he didn't want to leave her side, either—but General LaFayette needed him.

After a long embrace and kiss goodbye, James started for the college but stopped to watch Rebecca. She smiled and waved to him as she walked away. James waved back, waiting until she passed the Courthouse before continuing to headquarters.

When James returned to headquarters, General LaFayette immediately sought his input. "There is great need for a hospital for our sick," he said. "Where in town would you recommend we establish one, Captain?"

"The vacant Governor's Palace would suffice, sir," replied James. "There are three buildings well suited for the care of our troops. General Nelson used the advance buildings there as a hospital this spring."

"Well, we shall likely have need of the residence as well," replied General LaFayette. "Take Doctor Galt there and see if it is still suitable in its current state."

Doctor Galt, who had practiced medicine in Williamsburg with Doctor Pasteur, was the ranking physician in LaFayette's army. He already knew the Palace would serve well, but accompanied James anyway to see what needed to be done to transform the space into a proper hospital.

Luckily, all that was needed was to clean up the buildings, which had been vacant since May. Arrangements were made to do so and prepare them to quarter the sick and injured of the army. When Rebecca learned that the Governor's Palace was to be a hospital again, she immediately volunteered to help.

During the next week, everyone settled into a routine. James kept busy assisting General LaFayette with camp duties, and Rebecca reported to the hospital every morning to help with the growing number of sick.

General Nelson, who was still Governor of Virginia, arrived in Williamsburg on September 13th. He informed General LaFayette that he had come to command Virginia's militia, and that he required the service of Captain Southall to do so.

LaFayette transferred James back to General Nelson, who immediately tasked James with determining the number of militia who were in camp.

The next day, Williamsburg exploded with excitement at reports that General Washington and General Rochambeau were to arrive.

James, unaware that John was on his way to Williamsburg as well, described Washington's arrival to his brother in a letter he never got to finish.

September 15, 1781

Dear John,

General Washington and the French commander arrived here yesterday afternoon to much excitement. Twenty-one cannons fired a salute and great joy was expressed by the armies and the townsfolk.

It did not begin that way, however. They arrived around 4 p.m. in a carriage, without any pomp or parade, attended only by a few horsemen and Washington's own servants. They passed the militia camp before we were able to form, but word spread quickly, and the French troops and Continentals paraded in time to salute them.

I was with General Nelson. He and General LaFayette expressed great joy at General Washington's arrival. The Marquis clasped General Washington in his arms and embraced him with an ardor not easily described.

The artillery salute followed, and General Washington agreed to review the French and Continental troops. He has taken quarters at Mr. Wythe's house, and General Rochambeau, the French commander, stays at Mrs. Randolph's. Their troops are due soon, sailing down the bay and then up the river in transports.

Cornwallis may now tremble for his fate, for nothing, save some extraordinary intervention of his guardian angel, seems capable of saving him and his whole army from captivity.

James was called away by General LaFayette before he could finish the letter, and by the time he was able to return to it, there was no need to do so, for the very next day, on September 16th, John, Abigail, and Doctor Jenkins reached Williamsburg. They went straight to the Raleigh and surprised Mrs. Southall, who was ecstatic to see John.

Although business at the tavern was busy, the officers who dined there every evening were not allowed to lodge there; they had to return to camp in the evening. So John received his own bedchamber, while Doctor Jenkins and Abigail shared another.

James learned of John's arrival when their younger brother William arrived at headquarters just before noon with the news. Although the arrival of Washington the day before had sparked a lot of activity throughout the army, General Nelson released James for the rest of the day to visit his family. "We'll muddle on without you until your return in the morning," he said. James thanked him, then rushed to have Spartan saddled up, and the two brothers rode double to the Raleigh to see John.

Everyone had gathered in the dining room to pepper John with questions. He was laughing as James burst into the room and went straight for him. John rose as quickly as he could and greeted his older brother with a bear hug.

Mrs. Southall teared up at the reunion, and Abigail was touched at the display of brotherly love.

"James," John started, "let me introduce you to Miss Jenkins and her father, Doctor Jenkins. Abby, this is my brother, James—I mean, Captain Southall."

James shot John a quick frown, then took off his hat and bowed formally. Abigail returned the honor with a curtsey.

"I've heard nothing but good things of you, Captain. Your brother thinks very highly of you," said Doctor Jenkins with a bow.

"Yes, he does," agreed Abigail. "He talks about you often."

James smiled, then noticed John's cane. He ushered his brother toward a chair. "Sit, sit!" he insisted. "You must be tired after such a long journey."

The two brothers spent the next hour exchanging stories, then James proposed that John and Abigail join him to visit Rebecca. "She's at the hospital—the Governor's Palace. She volunteers there almost every day."

Abigail smiled at this.

"Yes, let's go and surprise her," John said excitedly. Doctor Jenkins offered to transport the party in his wagon and they all rode to the Palace. When they walked past the gate, they saw Doctor Galt just as he was about to enter the West Advance building.

"Doctor Galt! Good day to you, sir," James called. "Where might we find Miss Anderson?"

The doctor appeared flustered, but paused. "Good day, Captain Southall," he said. "She's in the residence in the back."

James led the party into the Governor's Palace and told them to wait in the hallway at the foot of the stairs. He continued into the ballroom, which had been fully transformed into a hospital ward. There were about forty sick men laying on cots, and there was Rebecca, tending to one of them, her back to the door.

James walked up to her and cleared his throat. "Miss Anderson," he said formally. "Could you please come with me?"

Rebecca whirled around, a mix of surprise, happiness, and then annoyance splashed across her face as she let out a sigh. "What is it, James? I'm busy," she scolded.

"You must come with me to find out," he said in an official tone.

"I really haven't the time," she complained, motioning to the other patients, but James continued to stand there, grinning like a fool. Rebecca sighed once more, but followed him toward the door. When James opened it, John was standing on the other side.

Rebecca's hands flew to her mouth as she let out a gasp. Then, before she could stop herself, before she could take in the cane, she rushed toward him and wrapped her arms tightly around him. James, who was just ahead of her to the side, helped steady John, who had nearly fallen from the impact.

"You're home! You're home!" Rebecca chanted with delight, still hugging John tightly, tears filling her eyes.

"I am," John laughed, patting Rebecca on the back.

Finally, Rebecca released him and took a step back to get a better look, beaming from ear to ear. "Oh, John! You're so thin, and—" she paused when she noticed the cane in his hand. "What's that?"

"Oh, just something I got at Ninety-Six," he said with a shrug. "Nothing to worry about. I have something much more important to show you."

He turned and waved Abigail and her father forward. "This is Doctor Jenkins," said John. "And this is his daughter, Abigail. They've taken good care of me while I was down South. I've written to you about them, though I'm not sure you received the letters."

Rebecca curtsied to both and they returned the honor. “I did, I did receive your letters,” she said. “It’s a pleasure to meet you both.” Then she looked directly at Abigail, her smile radiant. “Thank you,” she curtsied once more. “For taking care of John.”

Abigail curtsied back, dipping low to try and hide her scarlet cheeks. “It’s been my pleasure,” she said. “I am delighted to meet you, Miss Anderson. John spoke of you often. You mean a great deal to him.”

Now it was Rebecca’s turn to blush, but she didn’t let her embarrassment silence her. “So do you,” she replied. “He’s obviously quite taken by you, Miss Jenkins.”

John followed the discussion closely, praying that the two most important women in his life liked each other. It seemed that they did, but he wasn’t absolutely sure. Rebecca had surprised him in the past.

James cut through the brief tension and changed the subject, asking if Rebecca might join them for dinner.

“As it happens, I planned to go home for dinner today, but I’m sure my mother won’t mind if I join you all,” she said.

“Then ride back with us,” John said. “It must be about time for you to leave.”

Doctor Jenkins added, “Yes, take my seat in the wagon. I’d like to stay and see if I can help. I’ll walk back to the tavern in a few hours. I remember how to get there.”

“But what about dinner, Father?” Abigail asked.

“I’ll be fine. I’m sure I can eat something here.”

“It’s settled then,” said John. “Let’s head back, I’m starving!”

They took the wagon down the back street, and as they approached the brook Abigail yelled, “Stop! Stop! Is that the brook, John? The one you’re always talking about?”

“The very one,” he replied with a smile. “But we haven’t time to see it today. We can visit it tomorrow.”

They arrived at the Raleigh just before 3 p.m. Mrs. Southall had anticipated their return and had arranged for everyone to dine in the Daphne Room, next to the grand Apollo room.

Colonel Southall had learned of his son’s return and had left camp to join his family. John was the center of attention and was bombarded with questions throughout dinner. After much laughter, the dinner ended—but the conversation continued until dark.

Doctor Jenkins arrived at eight o’ clock, explaining that he had dined with Doctor Galt and then helped with some of the patients. "I shall report there regularly starting tomorrow," he said proudly. "I need to turn in now though, it's been a long day."

"We shall turn in, too," announced Mr. Southall, rising to leave. "I must return to camp early."

Mrs. Southall hugged James, and then John, whispering, "Welcome home, dear. We missed you."

John smiled and whispered back, "It's good to be home." He kissed her cheek. "Goodnight, Mother."

The stories continued in the Daphne Room with John, as usual, dominating the conversation. He avoided details of the many battles he was in, but eagerly described his fellow soldiers and some of his officers.

"General Morgan is everything you've heard he is. I've never seen an officer more comfortable with the men. We adored him! We felt that with Morgan in command, we could beat anyone. Just look at what happened at Cowpens against Tarleton. We crushed him!"

"What *is* it with you and Tarleton?" teased James. "It seems that all your battles were against him. Did you offend him somehow, before the war?"

John barked a laugh. “I wondered the same thing! I think he might have known that I escaped from Waxhaws and he couldn’t stand it.”

“James, what is General LaFayette like?” Abigail asked. For now, the conversation was light and joyful, but she remembered what John had been like after Waxhaws. She did not wish for him to return to that dark place.

Thankfully, John took the bait. “Oh, yes!” he exclaimed. “What is he like, James?”

“He’s quite remarkable. Just 23 years old and yet, he commands the respect of the entire army. He’s handled Cornwallis masterfully. We wouldn’t be here today without his leadership.”

“But what is he like as a person?” prodded Abigail.

“Well, it’s clear that he is French nobility, his manner and grace are exceptional. But he’s not arrogant like you’d expect nobility to be. He’s very charming and affable, and passionate for our cause.”

“Colonel Lee is a little like that,” noted John, describing Henry Lee of Virginia. Lee had developed a reputation as a dashing cavalry commander, and John said he lived up to every bit of the reputation.

The stories continued until almost midnight. The boys were impressed that Rebecca had faced down Benedict Arnold twice, and everyone was impressed by what John shared about Sergeant Collins.

Abigail hadn't met such notable figures, but her description of meeting John, and his deft ability with chamber pots, amused everyone thoroughly.

Once the laughter ceased, Rebecca stood, swaying a little. James rose to steady her, asking if she was alright. "Oh, yes, I'm sorry," she said. "It's just very late, and I'm a bit tired from my work at the hospital. I do wish I could stay longer, but—"

Abigail waved her off. "It is tiring work! I would love to talk more with you, but it is important you get your rest. And," she continued with a smile, "I am sure we will have many more opportunities to speak."

Rebecca smiled back. "Yes, you're right," she said. "It was a delight to meet you, Miss Jenkins. John is very fortunate to have made your acquaintance."

"The pleasure is all mine," Abigail replied. "I can see why John is so fond of you."

Rebecca looked to John. He was staring at Abigail with the same look she often saw James give her. She set her eyes back on Abigail, "I can say the same of you," she beamed.

Later, when everyone else had gone to sleep, James and John stayed up, continuing to talk. It was the first time in years that they shared a bedroom; it made them feel like children again.

"So, what do you think of her?" John whispered to James.

"Very charming, brother. I see why you are so taken with her."

John gave a great sigh—a happy one. It was too dark to see, but James knew John was smiling. "I am, James. I really am. She is just so wonderful. And she's done so much for me."

"We are all indebted to her. She has taken excellent care of you."

"She truly has." John paused a moment, unsure if he was ready to share this with his brother. He closed his eyes, then continued. "When I was…when I was injured," he said softly, his voice barely audible, "there was a moment where I wasn't sure I wanted to go on. If I *could* go on."

James went still, his breath caught in his chest.

“I was ashamed. I hated having to rely on others to do even the simplest things. I felt like a burden, and thought if this was what the rest of my life would be like… Well, then I wanted no part of it.”

James rolled to face his brother. “John—”

“Abigail suffered a very bad break when she was a child,” John continued. “It never healed properly, and so she walks with a limp now, and will, for the rest of her life. And yet…when I first met her, I never even noticed. I still have to look for it, and even then, sometimes I can’t see it. But she was just a child when that happened to her, when her life changed completely and she had to teach herself how to go through life in a new body. If she could do that and come out on the other side… Well, so could I. So, we walk. Every day. And she has me do all sorts of exercises and stretches to strengthen the muscles around my knee. It will… it will never be as it was.” He paused again, took a deep breath and then exhaled slowly. “But that’s okay. Just because it’s different doesn’t mean it’s bad.”

The brothers lay in silence for a while. James was unsure what to say, and John understood. He closed his eyes, and just as he was about to fall asleep, he heard James whisper, “She seems pretty special, John.”

John grinned. *Yes, yes she is,* he thought. He rolled to his side to face his brother. "She'd have to be to put up with the likes of me," he said with a laugh.

The next morning, Rebecca returned to the Raleigh, hoping to see James, but when she arrived, she learned he had returned to the militia camp at dawn. To help lift her spirits, John invited her to join him, Abigail, Doctor Jenkins, and the rest of his family for breakfast. They discussed the situation at the hospital, and Abigail, to no one's surprise, was determined to help out as much as she could.

Doctor Jenkins smiled, proud of his daughter. "We'll head over there after breakfast," he said.

"I'd like to help, too," announced John, surprising everyone.

But Abigail shot him a wicked grin and patted his arm. "Of course, John," she said. "Nobody empties chamber pots as well as you."

Rebecca was not expected at the hospital until the afternoon, but she decided to join the others and reported in the morning. She spent the time showing Abigail and John around.

Although the Palace no longer held its grandeur as the governor's residence, John was still thrilled to explore the entire building for the first time. "So many great men have walked these halls," he said, thinking more of Patrick Henry and Thomas Jefferson than any of the royal governors, "and now we're here."

"Yes, but I bet none of *them* had to empty a chamber pot," joked Rebecca, to Abigail's delight. "Time to get to work."

The sick and injured at the hospital were quartered in three areas, the former ball room, the large back room inside the main residence, and the East and West Advance buildings in front of the residence. There were about sixty ill soldiers in the hospital, with more expected as additional troops arrived in Virginia.

Rebecca and Abigail tended to the soldiers, checking on those with fevers, changing clothes and bedding when necessary, and cheering them up with a smile or kind word.

Despite Abigail and Rebecca's jokes, John's chamber pot days were over. He mostly visited with the patients, talking with those who were able, or just listening to those who needed an ear. He offered to write letters for some, but mostly he just listened as they described their families and homes.

As the days passed, John, Rebecca, and Abigail spent most of their time at the hospital. James, meanwhile, was busy with General Nelson and the militia. Their numbers had grown—as had the French and Continental numbers—when the troops from the north arrived on September 23rd. These new troops marched through town and encamped on open ground near the abandoned Capitol and in Waller's Grove.

The pace of preparation quickened for both the Americans and the British. General Cornwallis, now fully aware of the danger his troops were in, ordered his army to build more earthworks and strengthen those already in existence. And General Washington scrambled to collect the necessary equipment and supplies—especially food—for the two allied armies. With their number surpassing fifteen thousand men combined, it was a daunting challenge.

James accompanied General Nelson to several meetings at Mr. Wythe's house, which served as General Washington's headquarters. As James stood in the central passage of the house, he was flooded with memories of the kindness the Wythe's had shown him during his first year at the college. *It is good to be back here,* he thought.

"Captain Southall," Mr. Wythe called to him as he strode toward the central passage. "It is a pleasure to see you again, sir!"

"The pleasure is mine, sir," replied James with a bow.

Behind Mr. Wythe was General Washington, who heard the exchange.

"Captain Southall? Is this the lad I introduced to sweet bread all those years ago?" he said with a smile.

"No, sir. That was my brother, John. I am his older brother, James."

"Ah, yes. I remember you, sir. And how fares your brother?"

"He has just returned from South Carolina. He was wounded at Ninety-Six, sir."

General Washington frowned. "Yes, yes. A very unfortunate affair that one. If General Greene had had just a few more days…" He waved a hand, dismissing the thought. "Despite it all, he's managed quite well down there. Please convey my regards to your brother and parents. I had many an enjoyable visit to their tavern."

James nodded his agreement and Washington then continued into the parlor to join General Nelson and several other officers.

By the end of September, a mix of apprehension and excitement had settled in Williamsburg. John, James, Rebecca, and Abigail could all feel it as they strolled along the grounds of the Palace—one of John's many rehabilitation walks.

"I can't stay long," James said to everyone. "No one is to be away from camp tonight, so I need to be back by sunset. I think we'll likely march in a day or two. Everything appears ready and General Nelson said this would be my last visit. If the French navy can hold the British back, it's only a matter of time before Cornwallis is ours."

"That's grand, James," replied John, his voice tinged with a bit of envy. "I wish I could be there when they surrender. Tarleton is there, and after so many battles with him, I would enjoy seeing him surrender."

"The knowledge of his surrender will have to do," said Abigail, attempting to squelch any talk of John going to Yorktown.

"I just hope they *do* surrender," sighed Rebecca. "We've been disappointed so many times before."

"Yes, but we've never had so many troops *and* the French navy with us before," said John, choosing to overlook the failed Siege of Savannah two years earlier. "Cornwallis is doomed," he insisted.

"You just be careful, James. Don't do anything rash," warned Rebecca. "Stay with General Nelson."

"Must you remind me?" James chuckled. "In case you have forgotten, *John's* the rash one of the family. I'm the cautious one."

John punched his brother lightly on the shoulder in response, but everyone had a good laugh until it was time for James to say his goodbyes and return to camp.

Two days later, on September 28th, the American and French armies commenced their march to Yorktown.

Chapter Seventeen

Victory at Yorktown

Although the distance to Yorktown was just twelve miles, the warm, humid day took quite a toll on the troops unaccustomed to Virginia's climate. The march had commenced at dawn, but with over fifteen thousand troops, and all the baggage wagons required to supply them clogging the road, the two armies advanced at a snail's pace.

James and the militia brought up the rear of the column, which meant they didn't even begin marching until well after dawn. The frequent stops and starts of the long column annoyed everyone.

Leading the march was the French army, eight thousand strong. In the afternoon, just four miles from Yorktown, they peeled left, continuing toward the York River to ensure cover for the northwest approaches to Yorktown. Meanwhile, the Americans continued straight, aiming to block the southern and eastern approaches to Yorktown.

The terrain due west of Yorktown was a swampy morass, not passable on either side, and the York River—blockaded by the French navy—hemmed in the British from the north. General Cornwallis did have one thousand men entrenched across the river at Gloucester Point, however, ensuring that the Americans couldn't bombard Yorktown from there. Holding Gloucester Point also provided a possible avenue of escape for Cornwallis, should his situation in Yorktown become desperate.

The American army was delayed for several hours by a damaged bridge that needed repair and thus did not reach its planned camp location until after nightfall. The troops, including James and the militia, slept under the stars that evening, their tents still packed in wagons at the tail of the column. James heard scattered gunfire in the distance and figured nervous British sentries were to blame.

The Americans completed their march in the morning, and the militia had their tents pitched before noon. They were placed in reserve, behind General Benjamin Lincoln's and General LaFayette's divisions of Continentals.

James was relieved at their placement. *We will be well protected,* he thought.

General Nelson commanded all of Virginia's militia. Over three thousand of those troops were in camp with James, evenly divided into two brigades under Generals Edward Stevens and Robert Lawson. General George Weedon commanded another smaller brigade of militia across the York River in Gloucester County.

The scale of the allied siege of Yorktown was enormous compared to the one John had participated in at Ninety-Six, but the goal was the same: build a series of trenches and artillery batteries to shell the British, then move forward with zig zag trenches and build a second line of trenches and perhaps a third if necessary.

Before any of that could happen, however, General Washington and General Rochambeau needed to scout the British position.

Yorktown was ringed with twenty-foot-high earthworks that the British had hastily built in September. A number of cannons from the handful of British warships with Cornwallis had been added to the British works, but their largest cannons were only a few twelve-pounders. The rest were six and three-pounders, and then small mortars used to lob explosive shells at the enemy.

The firepower of the American and French armies was much stronger, with numerous twenty-four and eighteen-pound cannons, as well as twelve and six-pounders that they planned to use to protect their camps.

Cornwallis had over seven thousand troops with him, but many were sick, so his effective force was closer to five thousand.

The French and American armies each had around eight thousand men apiece. Some, however, had been left behind in Williamsburg, in case Cornwallis decided to launch a surprise attack there. And others were sick in the hospital at the Palace, but even with those men factored out, the allies still significantly outnumbered Cornwallis's army.

Time was of the essence for the allies, however, because the French fleet could not stay in the Chesapeake past late October. It had to return to the Caribbean to protect the French possessions there.

Time was also important to General Cornwallis, who needed to hold Yorktown until British reinforcements arrived from New York. In front of his main works around the town, he'd built a series of small redoubts to block each entry point to the town. The French and Americans would have to spend precious time attacking each of these redoubts before they could even begin their first siege line.

The day after the allied armies arrived outside Yorktown, General Cornwallis received word from General Clinton in New York that he could expect a relief force to arrive by ship within ten days.

When Cornwallis learned this, he decided to abandon his vulnerable outer works and defend just the main works encircling Yorktown. “If we defend the out works, the men inside will be sacrificed unnecessarily,” he explained to his officers. “We shall only keep the two redoubts on the river. Evacuate the garrisons of the others tonight,” he ordered.

When General Washington awoke on September 30th, he was stunned to find all the British outer works, except the two closest to the York River, abandoned. He immediately sent troops forward to occupy them.

“This is a most fortunate development,” James wrote to John. “It will speed up our progress significantly.”

John continued to volunteer at the hospital with Rebecca and Abigail. The patients were mostly ill, not wounded, although occasionally an injured man was brought in due to a mishap in camp with a wagon or ax.

By early October, however, the first wounded arrived, victims of skirmishes and British artillery fire.

Back at the militia camp, the days were spent preparing for the actual siege. Troops scoured the area for saplings and vines to make gabions, fascines, and other material used in siege warfare.

On the night of October 5th, James was accompanying General Nelson, who was with General Washington, when the American commander suddenly stopped and pointed out where the first trench line was to be dug.

James looked toward the enemy's position but couldn't see anything.

"The distance from the enemy will vary from six to eight hundred yards along this first trench," General Washington explained. "We'll begin digging just after nightfall tomorrow."

The militia did not participate in the start of the first trench; that honor belonged to the Continentals. Accounts of what occurred filtered back to camp and James described it to Rebecca in a letter.

October 6, 1781

Dearest Becca,

The noose tightens around our adversaries; we have begun our first trench line. The business was conducted with great silence and secrecy; the darkness of the night prevented the enemy from noticing our work. Hundreds of men advanced to the appointed spot that had been laid out by the engineers just an hour before. It is said that General Washington struck the first blow into the soil with a pick ax, and then the work party proceeded. They worked furiously all night, and by dawn had dug the trench deep enough that the long row of gabions placed in front of it—filled with the dirt from the trench—covered them from enemy fire. Up until that point, the British had been firing sporadically at us, seemingly unaware of our actions, but when they saw the new works in the morning, they started bombarding us with great intensity. We could hear the cannon fire in camp, and felt pity for the men in the trench, but learned afterwards that few were harmed.

The dispatch rider is leaving now so I must end this. I am sending it to the hospital, where I expect you will receive it by tomorrow. Until we meet again, I remain,

Your Loving and Affectionate,

James

Work on the first trench continued at a slower pace during the day because of the danger of more accurate enemy fire. Come nightfall, however, the work intensified once more.

General Nelson, James, and one third of the militia relieved the Continentals in the first parallel on the second night. Half of those sent to the first parallel formed a line of sentries about fifty yards in advance of the earthwork to guard against a sudden enemy attack. Those who remained in the trench worked hard on both sides to improve it. The ditch in front of the earthwork that had been started the night before was dug deeper, and the trench on the other side of the earthworks that protected the Americans was widened and extended. The dirt from both sides was piled on top of the earthworks, making them higher, thicker, and stronger. Other work parties constructed gun platforms for the cannons, which had yet to be brought up.

Siege of Yorktown

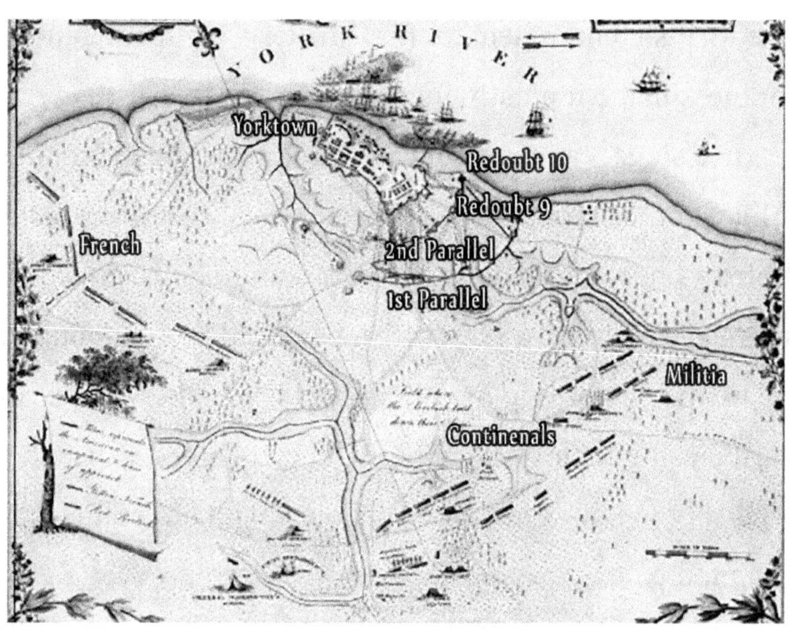

It was the first look at the trench line for James, and he was impressed at what had been accomplished in just one day. The British continued to fire artillery at them, but the darkness made it mostly ineffective.

In a siege, cannons typically fired two types of rounds: solid shot cannonballs to batter down earthworks and destroy opposing cannon, or exploding shells, to kill or injure enemy troops. The British had fired few cannonballs up to this point, saving them for when the Americans started using their own cannons. They planned to use their solid shot to knock out allied cannons with direct hits from a cannon ball.

Most of what the British fired at this point were shells, hollow iron balls filled with gunpowder. Shells were fired in an arc with a lit fuse, and if done properly, would explode over the heads of the Americans, or in some cases, amongst them as they worked.

Few British shells did so this evening. Most either exploded high above the Americans' heads—which was still a danger to the troops, but a much smaller danger—or burrowed into the ground and then exploded, muffling the effect.

James was captivated by the enemy's artillery fire. Each shot began with a flash from their lines, followed a second later by a boom. A shell arced across the night sky, its lit fuse creating a streak that was easy to follow. The streak usually ended with an explosion that reminded James of fireworks—just not as colorful, and *far* more deadly. Sometimes though, the shell was a dud and would plop harmlessly into the ground

The artillery fire lasted all night, unanswered by the Americans because they still didn't have cannons in the first trench, and they were out of musket or rifle range of the British.

James remained with General Nelson and the militia in the trench through the next day. They were relieved late in the afternoon by General Stevens, who had with him one thousand fresh militia. James and his section of militia returned to camp to rest, but the next day they were assigned to work details to build more gabions and fascines.

Two days later, James returned to the lines with the last third of the militia. The first parallel was largely finished, so most of their time was spent guarding the parallel under cover of the earthworks. The British maintained a gradual, but ineffective fire upon their trench and were finally answered in the afternoon by General Washington himself, who fired the first American cannon shot of the siege. Enormous twenty-four and eighteen-pound cannons blasted the British, much to the satisfaction of James and the militia, and the French added to the firepower from their section of the line.

The American barrage intensified in the evening. A British officer recorded in his journal that, "The whole night was nothing but one continual roar of cannon, mixed with the bursting of shells and rumbling of houses being torn to pieces."

A British naval officer assigned to duty in Yorktown estimated that, "Upwards of a thousand shells were thrown into the works on this night and every spot became alike dangerous." He added that, "The noise and thundering of the cannon, the distressing cries of the wounded, and the lamentable suffering of the inhabitants, whose dwellings were chiefly in flames…must inevitably fill every mind with pity and compassion who are possessed of any feelings for their fellow creatures."

The intensity of the allied bombardment surprised James. The satisfaction he'd felt when it had begun that afternoon had been replaced with pity for the targets of the cannon fire by the evening. *How can anyone survive that?* he wondered as he watched shell after shell explode upon the town and the two British redoubts along the river. He knew that the Nelson family had escaped long ago, but their home made a large target and General Nelson encouraged American gunners to aim at it.

"I don't want General Cornwallis to use it, so if it comes down, all the better," he declared.

With the first allied line fully operational, work began on zig zag lines extending toward the enemy. When they had advanced about two hundred yards, they began work on a second trench, just three to four hundred yards from the British works.

The British tried to hamper the allied effort, but had little success. James Thacher, a doctor with the American army, recorded in his journal that, "A tremendous and incessant firing from the American and French batteries is kept up, and the enemy return the fire, but with little effect.... We have now made further approaches to the town, by throwing up a second trench line...within about three hundred yards. This was affected in the night, and at day-light the enemy roused to the greatest exertions. The engines of war have raged with redoubled fury and destruction on both sides. No cessation day or night."

Although the British suffered mightily from the allied bombardment, they inflicted casualties upon the allies as well. James saw the result first hand when a party of militia were blown to bits by a shell that landed amongst them—just thirty yards from where he'd been standing. *Poor souls,* he thought as he stared at their shattered bodies. *They never knew what hit them.*

Rebecca, John, and Abigail also saw the result of the engines of war as more and more wounded came to the Palace. The wounded were treated at first in a field hospital, where amputations were a common remedy. Then, if they were lucky enough to survive, they were sent to the Palace in Williamsburg. Many were unresponsive when they arrived, still in shock at what had happened and what they had survived.

Rebecca and Abigail helped tend to their wounds, but John focused on trying to revive their spirits. It was a difficult challenge, one that prompted his own demons to reappear, but he never ceased his visits. He knew, more than he'd admit to the men he cared for, just how much they needed someone to talk to, to grieve with.

By October 14th, the American portion of the second line had advanced as far as possible. Two British redoubts blocked it from advancing further toward the river, and General Washington wanted those redoubts eliminated.

Shelling the forts hadn't worked, so he ordered a night attack. The French would attack the larger fort, dubbed Redoubt 9, and the Americans would assault Redoubt 10. Four hundred men from each army were assembled for the task, and they advanced toward the redoubts just an hour after sunset.

James was in the far end of the first trench, next to several large cannons. He watched as the Americans, commanded by Colonel Alexander Hamilton, advanced toward Redoubt 10.

The troops had been ordered not to load until they'd been discovered. Surprise was key, and Hamilton did not want anyone's musket to fire accidently. But when they reached the thick abatis laid out in front of the redoubt, British sentries heard them and opened fire.

The redoubt was manned by less than a hundred men, all of whom rushed to the walls to defend it. Hamilton's men charged forward, struggled through the thick abatis, tumbled down into the deep ditch at the base of the redoubt's walls, then, finally, hurried up the steep embankment.

There were flashes of British muskets and guttural shouts rang through James's ears, but it was impossible to determine which side was winning. Two hundred yards to the left of the American attack on Redoubt 10, the French struggled with equal intensity to take an even bigger redoubt.

After a few minutes, the sounds of fighting at Redoubt 10 ended. The struggle at Redoubt 9 raged on, however. *Did we take Redoubt 10? Is it ours?* James wondered, straining to see or hear anything that might reveal whether the attack had succeeded.

Finally, a messenger from Hamilton reached the line and announced that the attack had been successful. General Muhlenberg had already advanced with supporting troops. Now the militia was ordered from the first trench and began advancing toward the redoubt.

By this point, the fighting at Redoubt 9 had ended, and from the cheers and exclamations in French, James assumed they had been successful as well.

The militia with James and General Nelson carried gabions, fascines, and entrenching tools. Their task now was to incorporate the two captured redoubts into the second American parallel. But to do that, they needed to dig a connecting trench from Redoubt 9 to the American second parallel, two hundred yards to the left of the redoubt. A short trench connecting to two redoubts was also needed. Redoubt 10, which sat on the edge of a high cliff overlooking the York River, would anchor the right end of the extended second American parallel.

The militia went to work under heavy enemy fire. Allied cannons fired back, and in no time the night sky was filled with streaking shells and explosions. James stood alongside General Nelson, who never flinched as he urged the militia on, even when shells exploded nearby.

By dawn, the redoubts were connected to the rest of the American trench. Work to improve the new section continued all day, but by sunset the militia was relieved. James was exhausted and collapsed on his cot. He awoke at dawn the next morning to the sound of warning guns and drums. *They're beating assembly,* he thought. *What's going on?*

James helped get the militia into order, then reported to General Nelson. "The enemy attacked our trench last night and spiked a number of cannons," Nelson explained.

"It was just a raid though. It can't stop us, and the cannons will be repaired by the end of the day."

Nelson turned to General Lawson and said, "You can dismiss the men, General. The attack is over. There's no need for any more gabions or fascines."

The rest of the day passed quietly. In the evening, General Cornwallis attempted to evacuate his army across the river, but a violent thunderstorm swept in and scattered his boats.

By midnight, Cornwallis had reached a decision. He would ask for terms of surrender. The following day, October 17th, a British drummer appeared atop their earthworks facing the allies at 10 a.m. A British officer stood next to him with a white flag.

General Nelson and James were in the second trench checking on the militia assigned there when some of the men suddenly started shouting and pointing toward the British works.

"They're calling for a parley," said General Nelson, looking through his spy glass. "They want to surrender."

James was elated. When he returned to camp, he scribbled a brief note to John.

October 17, 1781

Dear John,

I think we've done it. Cornwallis has called for a parley and it's believed he will ask for terms of surrender. They've taken a terrible beating, so I am not surprised.

The big event we had hoped for appears here. The firing has ceased and the troops are joyous.

Please let Rebecca and Abigail know. I will write again when it is finished.

Your Humble Servant,

James

While negotiators between the two sides met behind American lines at the Moore House to finalize the terms of Cornwallis's surrender, John, who received James's note the next morning, urged Rebecca and Abigail to come with him to Yorktown to witness the grand event.

"It's what we've sought for six years," he stressed. "And it will be perfectly safe. James says the firing has ceased."

Rebecca and Abigail were both hesitant. "But we're needed here, John," Rebecca countered. "We can't just leave the wounded to fend for themselves." Abigail nodded her agreement.

But John would not give up. He continued to plead with them until they finally agreed to go. "But not until the morning!" declared Rebecca sternly.

"But—"

Rebecca crossed her arms, her brows raised in challenge.

"Fine," John huffed. "They're probably still negotiating anyway. But we must leave *early* in the morning."

"Fine," Rebecca said cooly, fighting to not roll her eyes—unlike herself, John had never been an early riser. "Abigail and I will be ready when you are."

Abigail bit back a smile as she watched John and Rebecca. Rebecca was sweet, there was no doubt about that, but there was a fire to her, too. *Perhaps that's what makes her hair such a lovely shade of red,* Abigail thought with a chuckle.

Doctor Jenkins allowed the group to use his wagon and just after dawn, John was in front of the Anderson's house with Abigail. They had to wait a few minutes, however, as it took Rebecca longer than she had anticipated to prepare.

At the last minute she had realized the trip would take the whole day and so had set to work preparing a basket of food to share with everyone.

To Rebecca's surprise, John did not mention her slight tardiness. "Good idea, Becca," was all he said when she emerged from her house with the basket.

I'm not sure I've ever seen him so excited, she thought with a smile.

John *was* excited. The girls could practically feel it radiating off him. "This is important!" he practically shouted. "If Cornwallis surrenders, I just don't see how the British can continue."

"It's been a long time coming," added Abigail.

"So many lives lost," Rebecca said sadly.

The group reached the militia camp before noon and found James with General Nelson in his tent.

"Ah, come to see the surrender?" Nelson asked when they'd been admitted into the tent.

John's eyes lit up. "It hasn't happened yet?" he asked.

"It's to happen this afternoon," answered James.

"Captain, we have some time. Take them to a good spot to observe it. But hurry back, we are to form up within the hour."

James led the small party to a hill overlooking the road to Yorktown and Hampton. "The British are to march from over there," said James, pointing toward the town, "And they will end up in that field over there. So, they will pass by right here. Our army will line both sides of the road."

"And where will you be?" asked John.

"I'll be with General Nelson and the other commanders on the field."

"Outstanding!" cried John. "You'll see Cornwallis hand over his sword."

"I expect so," replied James, "but I'll miss the whole thing if I don't get back."

"We won't see you afterwards," said Rebecca. "We need to get back to town."

James dismounted and reached out to lift Rebecca from the wagon. "Well then, I should give you this here," he said as he leaned in for a kiss.

Everyone was surprised by James's forwardness—most of all James—but he couldn't help it, something was in the air today. It had just felt right.

Rebecca was speechless when James pulled away, her fingers resting lightly on her lips. "I must be off," he announced briskly as he remounted Spartan. "It won't be long now."

James galloped away and John and Abigail climbed out of the wagon. "Guess he's excited," said John with a wry smile.

Rebecca's face was still red, but she was smiling. She feigned a cough and smoothed out her frock before finally lifting her eyes to John's. "Fetch the basket, will you?" she said. "We should eat while we wait."

While they ate, the American and French armies arrived, marching to the beat of their musicians. The troops lined up along both sides of the road, facing it. Soon after they had settled into position, the sound of drums thundered in the distance.

Rebecca heard the drums first and recognized the tune immediately. "It's the World Turned Upside Down," she announced. John and Abigail laughed.

"Very appropriate for the occasion," said John.

They were too far away to see faces clearly, but were impressed with the British and Hessians when they marched by. "Still professional soldiers," noted John. "Ramrod straight and disciplined to the end."

The troops marched on and on, five thousand in all, though hundreds of sick and wounded remained in Yorktown.

After about thirty minutes, with no end to the column in sight, the British suddenly stopped. "What's happening?" asked Rebecca, craning her neck to try and get a better look.

"I'm not sure," replied John as he squinted into the distance. "Maybe the officers are talking at the front of the column."

John was partially right. The British column had stopped because their officers had reached the place of surrender. They were led by General Charles O'Hara. He explained that General Cornwallis could not attend because of illness, an explanation that nobody believed.

James was positioned behind a row of generals and watched as O'Hara rode up to the French commander, General Rochambeau, and attempted to surrender his sword.

Rochambeau graciously waved him off and directed him to General Washington instead. O'Hara presented his sword to Washington, but he too waved off O'Hara and directed him to General Benjamin Lincoln, Washington's second in command. James was confused for a moment but then it clicked. *Good for you, General,* he thought with a smile. *Their second in command should indeed surrender to ours.*

It was an additional irony that General Lincoln was the one who accepted the surrender, since eighteen months earlier he had surrendered Charleston to the British. He'd been exchanged since then, and returned to the American army.

After the formal surrender finished, the long process of collecting the enemy's muskets began. The British and Hessian troops marched onto the field in sections and laid down their arms. They then moved off to the side to allow their comrades behind them to do likewise.

This would take several hours to complete and once John, Rebecca, and Abigail, realized what was happening, they agreed they should head back to Williamsburg.

"What a day," said John, as they all climbed into the wagon.

"Indeed," said Rebecca and Abigail in unison.

They reached Williamsburg just after dark and all three rushed back to their homes to describe what they had witnessed to their families.

Rebecca especially was in high spirits. She felt that this must be the final straw for the British. *Maybe this will finally end the war,* she thought as she drifted off to sleep, dreaming of American independence.

Chapter Eighteen

Adapt

Rebecca's dream would come true, but not for another eighteen months. The news of the British surrender at Yorktown electrified the American states and demoralized Great Britain and its leaders, who reluctantly began negotiations to end the war and recognize American independence. This would finally be achieved on September 3rd, 1783 when Great Britain and the United States signed the Treaty of Paris. Nearly eight and a half years after the Revolutionary War had begun at Lexington and Concord, and over seven years since the colonists had declared their independence on July 4, 1776, a new nation, the United States of America, was officially recognized and born.

While official American independence remained many months away, the city of Williamsburg was alight with optimism and joy. A week after the allied victory at Yorktown, James—who had been discharged from the militia—returned to Williamsburg and felt the change of atmosphere immediately.

And to think just a few months ago our city was occupied by the enemy, James thought, *families displaced and fearful for their futures.* He smiled at a family walking down Duke of Gloucester Street, attempting to chat with some French soldiers. Everyone was laughing, happiness practically radiated off them. James bowed to them as he passed, his smile widening, their joy contagious. *No one is afraid now,* he thought.

It had not been agreed upon before, but somehow James had known to go to the brook. Rebecca was there, chatting with Abigail, while John laid off to the side, a hat covering his face. *The lout,* thought James with a grin. *It's midday and he's asleep!*

Abigail spotted him first. She flashed him a smile, then leaned forward to whisper to Rebecca. Rebecca's head whipped sideways and before James could open his mouth to call out a greeting, she was upon him, arms squeezing the air from his lungs.

"It's been weeks!" she cried.

"One," James wheezed. "I'm sorry," he continued as Rebecca released him. "I meant to write, to return your letters. I kept expecting to be discharged, but our stay stretched on and on. I lost track of the time."

Rebecca dragged her gaze slowly up James's frame, her eyes narrowing when they finally locked with his. She had written to James twice during this period. Twice! She said nothing for a few more moments, enjoying immensely how tense James looked, then burst into a smile. "I'm only teasing," she laughed. "Of course things would have been busy. I knew you would return eventually. And besides," she turned to smile at Abigail and John, "I've had great company to keep me busy."

John was still lying in the grass, his face still covered by his hat. James shook his head and walked toward his brother, a finger pressed to his lips in warning. Abigail and Rebecca exchanged a look, trying very hard to suppress the laughter rising in their throats. "How great can the company be," James said, his voice gradually rising, "if it's asleep?" he finished with a yell.

John yelped and flung his hat sideways. James, Rebecca, and Abigail all burst into laughter. "Sorry, John," Abigail said between breaths. "James insisted."

John spread his arms over his head and gave a great yawn. “What do you mean?” he said, “I was just yawning is all.”

“Yes, because *that’s* what a yawn sounds like,” Rebecca snickered.

John stuck his tongue out at Rebecca, but laughed along with her. After retrieving his hat, he rose and greeted his brother with a hug. “Welcome home, brother.”

The four friends sat along the edge of the brook in silence for a while, enjoying the calming sound of the water.

It was Rebecca who broke the silence.

“For years I went to bed terrified,” she said softly, “absolutely terrified that I would lose you both to this war.” James placed a comforting hand on her shoulder, but said nothing. Out of the corner of her eye, Rebecca saw Abigail nod in understanding, and she could feel John’s eyes on her. “You are my very best friends,” she continued. “And… And, well, I—” her voice cracked and she swiped the tears from her eyes. “I am just glad we are all here. That you are still my very best friends.”

“We always will be,” James murmured, pulling her closer to him.

Rebecca smiled at him, then turned to Abigail and reached for her hand. "And I am so glad John found you," she said. "I cannot imagine a better person for him. You are truly a gift."

John nodded. "That she—"

"A *gift,*" Rebecca snapped, "John Southall. And don't you forget it!"

Abigail squeezed Rebecca's hand in thanks. "I am blessed to have met all of you," she said.

As the sun began its descent, the four friends watched as the sky transformed into vibrant hues of yellow and red.

"You know," John said, "even if I had died—"

"John Southall you shut your mouth!" Rebecca scolded. "I won't hear such talk!"

"Even if I had died," John pressed on, "our friendship would have lived on."

James nodded. "We would have never forgotten you, brother."

"Yes," Abigail cut in, "we would have made the pilgrimage each year, to this very brook, and laid down a chamber pot in remembrance."

The brothers exchanged a nervous look, then watched Rebecca carefully—her face was a mask, her lips pursed in a perfect O. But then, a shriek of laughter burst from Rebecca. She laughed so hard she clutched at her sides as if she were in pain.

The others joined in, laughing until tears streamed down their faces.

“It was an eventful year,” James said once his breathing had returned to normal and everyone had settled back down. He heard murmurs of agreement, but no one else spoke, so he continued. “When I first returned, I could feel it. The shift in the air, almost like an electrical charge—an excitement, a joy, but a nervousness, too. Things are going to change. They are *already* changing.” His voice dropped to a whisper. “Everything will be different.”

Everyone sat with the thought for a moment. It had been a year of turmoil and bloodshed, of fear and uncertainty. But it had also been a year of growth, of hope and love, of victory. It had not been an easy year for any of them. Yet, in many ways, it was a year they were thankful for—a year they would never forget.

Abigail sat between John and Rebecca. She reached for both of their hands, prompting Rebecca to reach for James’s. The four friends sat hand in hand, on the edge of the brook, the last rays of the setting sun shining on their faces. “Everything will be different,” she said. “But we will adapt.”

Heritage Books by Michael Cecere:

A Brave, Active, and Intrepid Soldier:
Lieutenant Colonel Richard Campbell
of the Virginia Continental Line

A Good and Valuable Officer:
Daniel Morgan in the Revolutionary War

A Universal Appearance of War:
The Revolutionary War in Virginia, 1775–1781

An Officer of Very Extraordinary Merit:
Charles Porterfield and the American War for Independence, 1775–1780

Captain Thomas Posey and the 7th Virginia Regiment

Cast Off the British Yoke:
The Old Dominion and American Independence, 1763–1776

Great Things are Expected from the Virginians:
Virginia in the American Revolution

He Fell a Cheerful Sacrifice to His Country's Glorious Cause:
General William Woodford of Virginia, Revolutionary War Patriot

In This Time of Extreme Danger:
Northern Virginia in the American Revolution

Second to No Man but the Commander in Chief:
Hugh Mercer, American Patriot

They Are Indeed a Very Useful Corps:
American Riflemen in the Revolutionary War

They Behaved Like Soldiers:
Captain John Chilton and the Third Virginia Regiment, 1775–1778

To Hazard Our Own Security:
Maine's Role in the American Revolution

Virginia's Continentals, 1775–1778: Volume One

Virginia's Continentals, 1778–1783: Volume Two

Wedded to My Sword:
The Revolutionary War Service of Light Horse Harry Lee

Williamsburg at War:
Virginia's Colonial Capital in the Revolutionary War

Witness to Revolution:
Growing Up in Williamsburg During the American Revolution
Michael and Jennifer Cecere

Witness to War:
The Sequel to Witness to Revolution*:*
Growing Up in Williamsburg During the American Revolution
Michael and Jennifer Cecere

Witness to Victory:
The Final Book of Witness to Revolution
Michael and Jennifer Cecere

www.ingramcontent.com/pod-product-compliance
Lightning Source LLC
LaVergne TN
LVHW020528100826
845148LV00010B/1384

9780788428586